Magic Oxygen
Literary Prize Anthology
2018

The writing competition
that created a charity

This is a First Edition of the paperback

Magic Oxygen Literary Prize Anthology:
the writing competition that created a word forest: 2018

By Tracey West & Simon West

Copyright © March 2018 Magic Oxygen

ISBN: 978-1-910094-61-7

eBook ISBN: 978-1-910094-62-4

Published March 2018
By Magic Oxygen
www.MagicOxygen.co.uk
editor@MagicOxygen.co.uk

Edited by Simon West & Izzy Robertson.

A catalogue record for this book is available from
the British Library.

Requests for permission should be addressed to:-
The Editor, Magic Oxygen
editor@MagicOxygen.co.uk

Printed by Lightning Source UK Ltd; committed to improving environmental performance by driving down emissions and reducing, reusing and recycling waste.

View their eco-policy at www.LightningSource.com

Set in 11.5pt Times New Roman

Titles set in Chunk Five

Contents

This Book is Dedicated to

The People of Boré, Kenya

For their indomitable spirit,
their hard work,
their resilience,
their ability to smile,
their warmth
and welcoming nature.

Friends of MOLP

Alex Katana Mare
working hard to pull everything together in Boré, Kenya

John Daniel Kadenge
an inspiring teacher in challenging circumstances

Izzy Robertson
supporting MOLP in too many ways to list

Helen Roberts
the constant provider of love, support, cake and stability

Simon and Elaine
for unwavering support and guidance with MOLP

Foreword

Ru Hartwell

We've got some good news and some bad news.

Let's get the bad news out of the way...

Boré is in many ways a typical rural and remote African community. The Giriama subsistence farmers who live there get very little support from outside agencies and with the drought currently afflicting East Africa showing little sign of abating, their predicament is not looking that positive, going forward. One of the biggest ironies of this situation is that the lack of rainfall that is making their lives so difficult is most likely caused by the climatic changes stemming from our voluminous carbon emissions up here in the developed world. To put it simply, these poor people are bearing the brunt of a climate whirlwind that they have had no hand in creating whilst in the temperate latitudes, where most CO_2 is released, most of us face few, if any, major impacts of global warming.

So now for the good news...

Luckily some rather clever individuals have created this unique entity called the 'Magic Oxygen Literary Prize'! What is so special about MOLP is that it enables people from the developed North, who are the ones causing the problem, to help out people from the less developed South who are 'picking up the pieces'. Every single writer who enters MOLP (and everyone who buys this book) pays for a seedling to be planted with a Kenyan school. MOLP's total impact is now running into thousands and thousands of new trees. They grow unbelievably fast down by the equator (up to 3 metres a year!) so each one mops up a big chunk of that problematic carbon dioxide, helps keep us cool and gives homes to countless tropical species from bats to baboons.

But that's just the beginning of the good news. The schools are paid to plant the trees and that money is used to build new classrooms which mean the kids can do their work out of the elements and can actually sit on benches at desks rather than on the bare earth. After only a few years the trees start yielding cash crops of timber, fruit and nuts which the schools can use to buy reading books, exercise books, paper, pens and rulers - all very highly prized resources that needless to say are desperately needed.

School enrolment is up, teacher morale is up, attendance is up. A virtuous circle of pupil achievement is becoming evident in these schools. More kids are going on to further education and fewer are going back to unsustainable charcoal burning. This means that not only are new trees being planted but ancient forests are being protected.

So creative writers from all over the world are helping budding young writers from one African community learn to write whilst creating new planet saving tropical forest. I'm just waiting now for one of the school children to enter and *win* the competition and that really will be a full circle!

Ru Hartwell
Director: Community Carbon Link
CarbonLink.org
BoreForestCentre.org
Trustee: The Word Forest Organisation
WordForest.org

Short Stories
Winners & Shortlisters

1st Prize - £1,000
My Name is Jennifer
by Joanna Campbell

2nd Prize - £300
Another Chance to Dance
by Jean Roarty

3rd Prize - £100
One Complete Moment
by Tannith Perry

Highly Commended - £50
Barbed Wire
by Hazel Atkinson

Highly Commended - £50
Somebody's Angel
by Margot Ogilvie

Shortlisted
Rosemary For Remembrance
by Valerie Bowes

The Moon is Always Escaping
by Chris Connolly

An Awfully Big Adventure
by Colleen MacMahon

Redemption
by Eileen Merriman

All for Ella
by Katy Wimhurst

Poetry

Winners & Shortlisters

1st Prize - £1,000
Orca
by Dee Barron

2nd Prize - £300
Cherries
by Judy Drazin

3rd Prize - £100
The Old Man's Grave
by Malcolm Deakin

Highly Commended - £50
Definition of a Tree
by Susan Rogerson

Highly Commended - £50
Mistook
by Jonathan Greenhause

Shortlisted
Daddy Longlegs
by John Harley

Transfiguration
by Neil Harrison

The Opera Glasses
by Michele Mills

Counting Backwards
by Lisa Reily

For My Father
by Nina Watson

Short Story Report

Beatrix Potter is reported to have said, "There is something delicious about writing the first words of a story. You never quite know where they'll take you." I agree with her wholeheartedly, but I would like to paraphrase her sentiment as a judge of MOLP. Thanks to Simon's technical wizardry, the entries appear, as if by magic, on my computer screen and each one carries with it a frisson of excitement as I'm never sure, as I start to read, exactly where it will take me.

On an adventure: of that much I'm sure. I know I will be moved, amused, astounded, shocked, scared and devastated in equal measure as I mark.

MOLP entrants are a fearless bunch, tackling just about everything under the sun and this year was no different; love, murder, bereavement, abuse, dystopia, fairy tales, disability and much more besides was served up to provide food for the judges' thoughts. I will confess to actually nearly burning the dinner once or twice because I couldn't drag myself away for long enough to give it a stir.

Judging is a fascinating and emotional process; as I writer myself I know just how much love, time and commitment has been poured into each piece and because there is such a breadth of style and subject matter, it can be hard to say that any one is better than another. No one on the judging panel takes the responsibility lightly; we all feel honoured to be asked. But it is a competition and so winners there must be. I would just like to say to those of you who didn't make it into this book, please don't feel disheartened; your entries, all of them, are what make this competition and the Word Forest in Boré, Kenya grows larger and more beautiful each year because of all of you.

The five entries that made the shortlist this year were, in author alphabetical name order, Rosemary For Remembrance by Valerie Bowes, The Moon is Always Escaping by Chris Connolly, An Awfully Big Adventure by Colleen MacMahon, Redemption by Eileen Merriman and All for Ella by Katy Wimhurst.

Valerie's Rosemary For Remembrance is consistently surprising. The characters are believably familiar and the simmering resentment and anger between them is cleverly underplayed. There's a wonderful simplicity to the writing of this nuanced tale. An otherworldly edge and a well delivered twist keep the reader on their toes all the way to the end.

Chris has created a haunting soliloquy in The Moon is Always Escaping, which takes us into the internal world of its central character and allows us to see an impossibly difficult situation from a rarely accessible viewpoint. A sense of claustrophobia, quiet desperation and desolation is all the more effectively achieved by spare, direct language. It will linger in the memory for days.

An Awfully Big Adventure is sweet and achingly sad. Colleen's ten year old narrator is utterly believable and I was very much swept away in her imagination, dreaming of adventure. The shadow that hovers over the family is adeptly illustrated from an unusual angle and the power of stories to protect us from the realities of life is brilliantly realised here. A poignant, thoughtful read.

From its chilling start to its frighteningly plausible ending, Redemption will keep you wondering. Internal and external dialogue carries the story along and the interplay between the two central characters is well crafted. A clever piece of writing, Eileen sustains an unsettling hint of menace through an apparently routine, if unusual, set of circumstances.

Imaginative and intriguing, All for Ella brings a quirky dystopia vividly to life. Katie conjures up a feast of images in a delightfully humorous way, deliciously underscored by the darkness requisite of the genre. Warning - you will never regard the Lottery in the same way again!

We now reach the top five prize winning entries. Barbed Wire by Hazel Atkinson and Somebody's Angel by Margot Ogilvie both scooped £50 and a highly commended accreditation. Tannith Perry took third place and won £100 with One Complete Moment. In second place, winning £300, was Another Chance To Dance by Jan Roarty while first prize and

£1,000 was awarded to My Name is Jennifer by Joanna Campbell.

Barbed Wire is stark and raw, yet at the same time incredibly rich and utterly gripping. The complex relationship between the two main characters is exquisitely drawn, the narration adding layer upon layer of emotional depth. Brutality and tenderness collide as Hazel explores loss, guilt and the search for redemption in a courageous and delicately nuanced story. This will break your heart but the ending is a beautifully wrought shimmer of hope in the darkness.

The two situations in Somebody's Angel are apparently almost the opposite of one another and yet, as the story unfolds, come from a remarkably similar root. Margot has skilfully juxtaposed them to create a beautifully rounded and emotional journey for the reader. Some serious and difficult themes have been addressed in a genuine and heartfelt manner, with beautiful control of pathos and touching sensitivity.

In One Complete Moment Tannith's elegant use of language brings a dystopian future vividly to life. The narrator's nostalgic lifestyle is neatly counterpointed by the harsh sterility of the outside world; evocative description and a wonderful eye for detail allows us to see both. It's impossible not to empathise with her as she mourns for past times and fights against the inevitable advance of 'progress'. This story will leave you re-evaluating many of the things we take for granted.

Another Chance to Dance compassionately handles circumstances in which no-one would want to find themselves. The characters are all the more sympathetic for their ordinariness and Jan puts us neatly into the shoes of the narrator, allowing us to see her disabled mother so clearly. The power of this piece lies partly in the simplicity with which it is told; short lines and a 'matter of fact' style work most effectively to convey the conflicting and desperate feelings of the daughter, and I was on that emotional rollercoaster with her the whole way. This is masterful storytelling; have tissues handy.

My Name is Jennifer is a period piece set in World War II. Joanna places us effortlessly in the narrator's world; Jennifer's voice is clear and direct and leads us through a multi layered tale of everyday horrors and courage in adversity with no frills or extraneous embellishments. The characterisation is skilled, with terrific attention to detail. Clever and consistent use of a colloquial style with unusual and vivid description keeps the pace beautifully even and some unexpected twists are masterfully accomplished. Although I was reading, it felt more as though I was listening to Jennifer speaking. This will have you well and truly hooked and you won't be able to help cheering quietly for the heroine at the end. An outstanding piece of writing and a very worthy winner.

It's been a pleasure to review these wonderful stories; now it's your turn to make yourself a cup of tea, sit down for a while and enjoy them for yourself.

Izzy Robertson
Judge

Joanna Campbell
England
1st Prize - Short Story

Joanna is a full-time writer from the Cotswolds. Her novel, Tying Down The Lion, was published by Brick Lane in 2015 and her short story collection, When Planets Slip Their Tracks, by Ink Tears in 2016.

Her stories have appeared in all kinds of anthologies and literary magazines. Her short story, 'Upshots', won The London Short Story Prize in 2015 and in 2017 her novella, 'A Safer Way to Fall', was a runner-up in The Bath Flash Fiction Novella-in-Flash Award. Her flash fiction piece, 'Confirmation Class' won second place in the 2017 Bridport Prize.

See more at joanna-campbell.com

My Name is Jennifer

Dinner time, the bomb drops round the corner. Like the sky has split itself.

The ceiling light shudders. Mam's lumped out the mash and she's about to cut into the rabbit pie, but the knife crashes onto the plate.

I'm at home with earache, a daft plug of iodine holding in the pain, elsewise I'd be at school, with the explosion.

We burst our lungs hurrying to the shelter in the back yard, Mam's apron strings streaming. She's hugging our lad tight. I'd sooner finish the pie, to be honest, and take me chances. Mam made the pastry dead pale and soft. You shouldn't bite on hard things with earache, she said. By heck, when Big Wally's not here, she's exactly how a mam's meant to be. When he is here, Mam's more brittle than scorched moth-wings. When he buggers off home later, she flits back out like a red butterfly in summer.

In the shelter, she sobs her guts out and the babby turns purple and sticky with bawling. I'd tell 'em to pull theirselves together, but they'd not hear me, so I hold their hands.

At the all-clear, we stumble back to the kitchen, where Big Wally's wolfing the cold pie with a big china-faced doll in a bridal gown.

He snatches up our lad, swinging the poor little bugger about when I've only just got him off, then soon as he tires of it, drops him back in the pram.

"Bomb dropped right on the school," he says.

Mam asks him, "Did anyone…?"

"No one," he tells her.

Thank the Lord God Almighty. Not that I'm the praying sort, mind you, but some bugger up there's got to be listening, hasn't He?

According to Wally, the china doll were staring up at him from the bashed-about benches, amid a million scattered book-pages and the hard-arsed vaulting-horse thrown wrong side up.

"Finders keepers," he says, grimy fingers flicking at her finery.

War raises the bad streak in folk like a welt. It's livid in Wally, the gleam of greed. He reckons you can't trust folk over ten years old. He sends youngsters to bombsites to pick shillings from gas meters. Shelling whelks, he calls it. Fleecing folk dry, I'd say. Not to mention robbing kiddies of their decency.

He peels clothes from dead bodies. Slices off fingers with a vegetable-knife, helping hisself to the rings. Last summer, he showed me one in his pocket. Not the ring—that were long gone—the finger, rolled up in a handkerchief.

I stopped meself spewing up. Don't know how. Just swallowed hard. What else can you do when a finger's pointing at you all by itself? I'd never show him I were scared. He'd die laughing. By heck, happen I should.

I know this china doll though. And it's not his to keep.

"Half her poor face is cracked wide open, look," Mam says.

"Don't want to look," I tell her, turning away to jiggle the pram. Our lad's dropped off on account of the sugar Mam adds to his bottle. Nigh-on half a week's ration she's tipped in.

"Beggars can't be choosers," says Wally, thudding hisself onto a chair, great tub of lard that he is, elbows oozing over our table. "She'll fetch summat at market like-as-not."

I've never ruddy well begged him. But I don't say owt. Too scared. More scared in me own house than I'd be walking the streets in an air-raid with a bright-faced torch and Up yours, Adolf painted on me beret.

Grey powder cakes Big Wally's hair and clogs his throat. He splutters for show into his hanky, then unfolds his cap from his pocket and thumps it hard between his hands, raising ash-clouds that trail inside the sunbeam crossing the table, then float onto the plates.

"Plane flew off course, folk are saying," he says, clapping the cap in half and stuffing it back in his pocket. Tipping hot tea from his cup into the saucer, he slurps.

"They didn't mean to bomb the school then?" Mam asks, as if this makes the news better, like a drop of syrup in brown medicine.

"Jerries don't care what they hit," he says.

He's not bothered neither. Summat-from-nowt's all he cares about.

"Think on, Mam," I say, holding her hand while she stares at the cup of tea I've put in front of her. "If it weren't for the earache, I'd have been there."

"Well, there's no one there now," Mam says, stroking Wally's wire-wool hair. Black flecks flutter out and pepper his tea dregs.

Daft beggar, she is. 'Course they're all there. Busy tidying up. It'll be home-time soon, but the teachers'll stay on, get the brooms out, shift the vaulting horse back up again, carry the benches inside, glue the books together.

"I missed it all, Mam," I say, patting her hand.

"Pipe down, you. Your mam's upset," says Big Wally. "She could've been pushing the pram to the shops. Stuff were flying out onto the pavement. She might not be sat-sitting here now. Nor the babby."

"Would the pram have kept the lad safe d'you think, Wally?" Mam asks, tearful.

"Happen. Happen not."

Her face caves in, like it's melting, and Wally tells me, "Look what you've gone and done," then guides her like she's a blind woman into the front-room.

When Dad were alive, we only used it for Sunday dinner, Christmas dinner and blood relatives. The rest of the time, to shield the furniture from the sun, the curtains are kept pulled together. I don't know how Wally comforts her, sat in the half-dark. Don't care to know.

I sit the doll up in the pram with our lad, her soiled dress spreading round her like a pool of gone-off milk.

"By 'eck, I know you. Mrs Harvey brought you in to show us. Dead classy, in't she, Mrs H? Them lacquered fingernails, shell-pink. Happen she paints it on her toenails 'n all. That's how you can tell a person's classy. They paint what's not on show."

Mrs H made the doll's frock from a snippet of her wedding dress, which were cut from a pair of her auntie's net-curtains. There's no photographs, what with her groom having to hurry back to the fighting. And what with her sister needing a christening frock, the dress were cut up straight after the do. So we'll never know how Mrs H looked on her special day.

"I couldn't resist making my doll a dress from the last remnant," she told us. "I should have used it for something useful, but I so wanted a reminder." That's how she talks. Dead posh, in't she?

She went on about make-do-and-mend, being thrifty and all, but after the girls had passed the doll round—the boys wouldn't touch her—Mrs H sighed and said, "Sometimes, you need something purely for your own self. Something personal."

I couldn't help meself gawping at the water-soft lace and the porcelain face and the shiny, flushed fingernails. Dead pure, dead personal.

Our lad's stirring again, thumping his podgy great legs. Little toe-rag, he is, turning up out of nowhere, skriking half the night and making us dog-tired. Mam's dead scared of him. She's tied a bit of lard on a string knotted to his cardi so he can suck on it and fatten hisself up even more. There's two reasons why.

Firstly, she hates his guts. To make up for the guilt, she pretends he's God's Gift and spoils him. And second of all, what with him being born out of wedlock, she's terrified of God's wrath hammering down. She were already sinning summat chronic, you see, on account of Big Wally having hisself a wife in Gas Lane. He's Walter to her and Wally to Mam, so he can always tell where he is. Half his time for his missus, half to us. A foot in each camp, so to speak. One of these days, he'll split his ruddy trousers.

So what with the war on 'n all, pure pleasures—like jam—are spread thin. And I've nowt you'd call personal, as it happens, what with our lad's great iron cot taking over me bedroom, the nappy bucket stinking out the scullery where I used to hide with me books, and Big Wally treating the place as his own. As for Mam, there's only the scraggy leftovers of her.

Leastways I've got school, what's left of it. Where's me hat? I'll go and give them a hand. Better than staying here to see Mam coming out the front-room flushed as a pickled beet and her neck more bruised than a rotted apple. Happen I'll take the doll with me and give it back to Mrs H. By 'eck though, what'll Big Wally say when he sees it gone?

I sit her on the pram with our lad tucked inside and inch through the hall, quieter than a dormouse in winter, but the bad wheel squeaks anyroad and Wally calls out, "Gerrus an ounce of Virginia," before he goes back to his rough, fast breathing.

I'm sweating conkers. I can't do this, can I?

Can I?

Sod it, I'll tell him someone stole the doll off me. He'll still give me what-for, but I'll not let Mrs H down.

I trundle the pram down the road, the wind badgering the new leaves and the sun sending their shadows jittering over the pram hood. Without the racket of four o'clock home-time, an eerie peace settles on the afternoon.

I'm steeling meself for some mess, but according to Wally, the place is still standing. Just the windows blown out and the furniture sent flying. Anyroad, the dinner hall's separate, at t'other end of the playground, shielded by a great row of sycamores. It must've escaped a direct hit because Big Wally said nowt about anyone being hurt.

Did anyone…?

No one.

From here, you'd never know owt's happened, apart from a twist of smoke dirtying up the sky. I'll tell Mrs H the doll were taken by mistake. She'll not believe it, but she'll say nowt. Everyone knows about Big Wally. No sense in mithering over what can't be changed. Stuck with it, aren't you?

I park the pram outside the school gates. There ought to be a name for the stench of wet soot. And for the aching sound of rubble crackling underfoot.

The heavy-rescue fellas in their oilskins and helmets are packing up their tools. There's the bricklayer who mended our wall when the rag 'n bone man's horse crashed into it and the plumber who came to stop the flood from Big Wally smashing Mam's head against the kitchen tap.

"Glad you weren't here for this, Jenny," says Bob Acreman, who does electrics. He's the type who looks through all that's in front of his nose and fixes what's beneath. Happen that's why he's handy with wires and such. "Go careful now. We've made it safe, but you'll have to watch it."

I climb up a mountain of shattered timbers and bricks. It shifts beneath my feet and Bob has to steady me.

"By heck, it's still there!" The words fly out of me like streamers from a magician's mouth.

The school building is in one piece, the glass smashed as Wally said, but the roof on, the walls standing, the ivy still climbing.

"Best look yonder, love," Bob tells me, dead weary. He takes off his helmet and bows his head, as if he's in church.

The sycamores are heaving, getting theirselves flustered as the wind gusts up. Their branches are choked with black wreckage. A tree's fallen on the building, its colossal, witchy-fingered roots clawing the air. The dust-haze is bluish, as if we're in the middle of a heatwave, and there's a million broken bits of china, the two big ovens lying on their sides, and the smell of cremated food.

"The roof was smashed in, Jen. The walls burst open and the whole thing just buckled and folded itself up."

"So where is everyone, Bob?"

He answers straightaway, not even sighing first, his kind hand closing over my shoulder as if it's a poor, dead bird.

"Trapped, Jen. We moved careful, in case anyone called out. But no one did."

The smouldering rubble stinks of Sunday crackling. There should be a name for it.

Did anyone...?

No one.

Don't need me to fill in the blanks, do you?

"The morgue's in the community hall," Bob says.

By heck, so fast. When you think about it, they take no time, do they, all the important things: a couple wed, a baby made, a school gone.

"Your day off, was it, Jen?"

"Aye. And now I've no days on, have I?"

Last year, I had to take a month off. They let me come back though. Not as a pupil, but as an Assistant. Capital A, since it were official-like. I weren't on Pay-Roll, but I had a Position. Mrs H put in a good word because she knows—she knew—about needing summat for yourself.

Our lad's wailing. I shake off the powdery dust smothering his blanket. I think about him all the time, you know, like I'm thinking now about everyone caught by the bomb, but I don't feel owt. For a twelve-month, I've been thinking, without feeling. And sometimes it's even like someone else is doing the thinking, and I'm left behind somewhere. But now, with the school's blank windows staring and the afternoon crows gathering, with no slamming of desk lids, no pounding of sandals, no babble of mams around the gates, I can't think anymore.

I take the doll off the pram and pick up the babby. It's an armful to juggle, but I manage, needing the heat and weight of them in me arms.

Bob's putting on his helmet again, back to business. Helped by the other men who never stop working, he probably chased off Big Wally, the doll already slid inside his donkey-jacket.

"Going over the community hall now, are you?" Bob asks me.

"Aye, in a minute. Can I go in the classroom for a bit?"

"It's safe enough to step inside. I'll stand at the door."

The smoulder has drifted in, but the smell of chalk and damp plimsolls is hanging on. I go careful, what with the crunchy floor shifting, my heart pumping fit to bust and our lad struggling. I'm glad of it though, glad of his kicking feet, his boneless little arms.

"All I feel is shame," Mam said when he were new-born. She wouldn't hold him, not for weeks, and when she did, it were nowt to do with love.

In Mrs H's classroom, the door's lolling off its hinges, but the stripe of afternoon light still slants along the floor. Her desk and chair have gone. I sit the doll on a piece of broken blackboard, arrange the dress nicely and drape my hanky over her head, to make a veil over her gaping wound. It's a bit of a job, what with hanging onto our lad 'n all, me ear bad and me stomach growling for food, but don't go thinking I'm having a moan. I'm only blethering on so I don't cry.

Don't cry.

I've not wept for ages. And it wouldn't be right to start today.

Don't start, you.

I swallow hard and when Bob says it's time to go, I give him a nod. You can't say owt when your throat's jammed with a twelve-month of tears. Anyroad, we've had a ruddy bomb dropped. There's no words for summat stronger than you, louder than you, almightier than you.

The community hall is a place of quiet pain. There's nowt the mams can do except say goodbye for the last time, so they can't leave. Dads arrive, pushing past me, white-faced. Small kiddies are crawling about, hands slapping the floor. Someone's set up the tea urn at the back.

Folk ask me why I'm alive. I don't say owt. It's not right saying I stopped at home with a bad ear. If only, if only, they'll all be thinking.

They'd sooner I were lying on the floor too, a coat over me face. I'm a disgrace round here. Most of 'em were vexed about Mrs H making me Assistant.

Bob's wife, Marjorie, hands me a cup of tea. She's not lost anyone. She's here because she's a good woman. She takes our lad from me and says I'm to sit down. All the chairs are along one side, opposite the row of children and teachers.

27

I can't help counting 'em. Three times I do it. I count whenever I mustn't cry. I've counted to thousands and back again.

"That's not everyone," I tell Marjorie.

"No, not all of them's here," she says.

Not all here? Happen Mrs H is manning the urn. I'll see her any minute. Oh, please, Lord God Almighty, let her be here.

"Where are the others then?"

"Well...nowhere, I'm afraid, dear. There's some that were...quite gone."

All that's left is the row on the floor. I could tell who's who if they still had their shoes on, but you never see folk barefoot, do you? The shoes found in the muddle have been piled into a coal sack by the door, for taking home.

Marjorie carries our lad off, making it her mission to find him a drop of milk. "At least I can do something for this poor lamb," she says.

I've not been near the community hall since last May. We gathered here after a trip to the seaside so Mrs H could dish out the picnic leavings, half a bun or a hard-boiled egg to take home. I were nut-brown, my hair sun-yellow. Mams swarmed everywhere, tucking sandy spades under their arms, lugging tired children home. I were the last to leave, me bucket rattling with warm crab-casts and limpets. I were old enough to go home by meself. But Big Wally had said he'd come and get me.

He came. He got me. Outside, at the back. In the cat-piss weed. I were His if He said so. I were Nothing. I weren't to breathe a word.

I kept counting, to five thousand and back again. Aye, it took that long, all told.

No crying now.

We all had summat to take home. No one else had what I got.

It were Bob Acreman who found me. The harebells were still blooming, their mauve mist and touches of green flitting past as he carried me to theirs in his arms. He and Marjorie asked, of course, who it were, but I were told to say nowt-or-else. So I said nowt.

It were Marjorie who helped me break the news to Mam about our lad being on the way. I said it were a fella from the funfair who did it. Said he worked the dodgems. I dressed him up that much he were all but real to me. I gave him red curls.

I'm shivering now. My tea slops into the saucer. It seems dead rude, but it's hard not to look at the row of bare feet. One pair of ankles is cobwebbed with wispy nylon tatters.

I walk across to them and kneel down. As soon as I hold her feet, the tatty stockings flake off. I spit on my hanky and wipe the two big toe-nails, then all the little nails.

There, I said, didn't I? Shell-pink, they are. All ten. Right classy. I give her feet a rub, but they're made of stone. They'll be no warmer, but I'm doing it for meself, to be honest. Pretending to help is better than nowt.

"Think on, Mrs H, you'll always be a bride," I tell her. "It's still your wedding day, you could say, on account of Mr H having to hurry back to the war. You're pure. You won't never have to push out a babby. By heck, that takes a lot of counting. Ten thousand and back again."

Marjorie hands me back our lad. She's rocked him to sleep.

"Bit grubby, isn't he Jenny?"

"Aye. It's the lard. Stills him, Mam says."

"Oh, she shouldn't." Marjorie clicks her tongue. "Look, Jenny. I know this isn't the time to say it, but you know we've not been blessed with our own. We'd take him for you in a flash."

"He fits me arms better now you've rocked him," I tell her. "He's warmer and softer. Happen I'll take him into me bed tonight."

It doesn't sound like me, on account of its me insides doing the talking now, spilling out-like.

"Let him be a comfort to you, Jenny."

"More than I'll ever be to him, like-as-not."

"Well, although I'd have him in a heartbeat, I'd say all he needs is you, dear. You're the best in the world to him."

A heartbeat, a flash. Long enough to flatten a school, to lay my teacher in a morgue, to replace her with her own doll, to know there's no one up there listening. And to feel summat, after all this time.

Back at home, I park the pram in the kitchen. Hark at Wally, shouting for his baccy. The daft sod can wait.

I scoop me laddo out of the pram and tell him, over and over, "Your mam's here, Jimmy."

I called him Jimmy after me da, or happen it were mostly to vex Big Wally.

When Wally banged the cinders out of his cap, he filled the kitchen with the poor, dead folk from the school. They're settling here now.

This house is what you'd call their final resting place. I'll not see them again, but they can't leave us.

Earlier on, I wished I were one of them. Now, I feel almost lucky. Dead strange, it is. A torment and a relief both at once. There should be a name for it.

There should be a name for the bristle-weeds growing out of a fat fella's string vest. And a name for someone dead bad who swings his lad in the air to make him smile. And a name for the solid heat of your babby's head crammed in the crook of your neck, his milk-sweet breath glazing your skin.

Talking of naming things, here's a start. I'm not Nowt. I'm Jimmy's Mam. And I'm the Assistant. Don't forget the capital A. I'll show you all, one day me and Marjorie will put the school back to rights, ready for Jimmy and the other small ones what's left.

And I'll show Big Wally.

His donkey jacket's still slung over the chair. I take his handkerchief out of the pocket, unroll it and pick up the yellow, waxy finger. And I bite it.

Not just scraping, namby-pamby, with the edges of me teeth neither. I sink 'em in, deep and hard, all the way through, until the whole thing fills my mouth.

There. Told you. He's a steaming great liar. I've proved it. And if he ever dares point owt at me again, I'll bite straight through that 'n all.

It's nowt but marzipan. Which is another name—same as treacle, syrup, or jam—for summat soft and full of sugar. Same as Wally's just a name for a fella full of shite.

Me earache's gone. I'm taking out the cotton-wool now. Happen I'll put it in Wally's tea later. My name is Jennifer, I'll tell him. Capital J. And I'll not answer to owt else.

Jean Roarty
Ireland

2nd Prize
Short Story

Another Chance to Dance

A single leaf pirouettes downward, landing at my feet. I stare at the golden corpse of what was once summer. Then I stab in the door code. Margaret is on reception today.

"Hi, Deirdre," she says, handing me the pen.

All the staff know me. I've been coming here for years. Since Mother's admission, a host of residents have died. I envy their relatives. The visitor's book lies open on the desk: *Visitor's Name, Resident's Name, Time In, Time Out.* I no longer write her name. She is number 42. The clock on the wall says 11.30, but I write 11.25, always shaving a few minutes on the way in then adding a few minutes on the way out. I press the gel dispenser. The fresh-scented, soothing liquid is a welcome delay.

I will be glad in an hour, when, if it's a good day, I'll wheel Mother to the dining room and escape. Then I will flee downstairs, sign out and run towards life: do the shopping, go to the bank, collect Jenny from school, cook dinner and work my evening shift. There are times when I indulge in thoughts of the deliverance Mother's death will bring.

The lift takes me up to the second floor. Sometimes, by mistake, I end up on the third, which is exclusively for Alzheimer's patients and has keypads everywhere. Mother does get confused, especially when she has an infection. Who wouldn't after years in captivity? It's her body, though, that's the problem. She can move her arms a bit, but the rest of her is paralysed. Years ago, we promised to help her die if things got really bad. That plan helped her live. She wanted to dance into death, to die living, she said, and not die dying.

I brace myself before heading down the long corridor to her room. Ever since she came here we visit every day to keep on top of things. Unanswered call bells ring incessantly. The corridor smells – that awful nursing home smell. It bends to the right where a wall of glass lets in a flood of early autumn light. I watch dead leaves, whorl into mini tornadoes, then quiver as the wind eases. They gather in a heap in one spot of the flower bed, the way dust favours one corner of my hall.

My heart lightens when I peep inside the room. No sign of her. The days when she's bedbound due to illness, spinal fractures or pressure sores are the worst.

Her pain is my pain.

I hasten to the day room. Amongst the lines of elderly women and men I see her slumped body – a white-haired shell, trapped in her wheelchair. I go over and hug her bony frame. Her sunken eyes sparkle.

"I'm so glad you came, Deirdre."

"I'll get them to straighten you up, and we'll have a cup of tea."

It's like we have switched roles and I'm the mother.

On the far side of the room, I spot her friend, Janette, and wave to her. Mother's arms are weak, but she can manage to propel her wheelchair slowly. When she's confused or overwhelmed by pain and powerlessness, she ends up in Janette's room. Janette looks out for her. When I bring in mint sweets, I always leave a second packet inside Janette's door.

Take the child by the hand, take the mother by the heart.

"Hang on just a sec, Mother," I let go of the wheelchair's ridged handles and make my way over to Janette, kneeling in front of her to say a quick hello. My knees crunch as I bend down.

"Pull over that chair," she says, gesturing towards an empty one.

"I can't stay."

Janette sighs, disappointment crossing her face. She leans forward. "Just to let you know," she says. "Your mother's gone off mints."

"Has she?" I smile.

"Yes. Maybe bring in toffees for a change."

In my peripheral vision I see Mother trying to move her wheelchair towards the door as if asking to leave. I nod in her direction. "Looks like we're off. Thanks for the heads-up about the toffees."

Before I get to her, she has already crashed into Jim's armchair. He doesn't notice. I manoeuvre her out and we go to her room. We park in her usual spot – near the door and within reach of the little shelf unit. She likes the door left open, through which the muffled sounds of the day room TV can be heard. I rearrange items on the shelf to make room for the tray, move the jewellery-draped Statue of Liberty back against the wall, and shove the dusty glasses case, sticky protein drink and kidney-shaped sick bowl out of the way.

"Are you warm enough?" Her red nylon blouse looks a little flimsy. "Will I get you a cardigan?"

"I'm okay."

The blouse clashes with her faded purple skirt. The yellow knee socks aren't hers. She rolls her wheelchair nearer to the shelf. Her rigid legs, like locked hinges, fall awkwardly to one side, and her feet hang off the foot rests. I reposition her legs. Her long shin bones jut against my hands. Finally, I force her feet into place, careful of the broken skin that bleeds from her heels. A lifetime ago those feet danced their way to an All-Ireland Ballroom title. The foxtrot was her forté. We loved to watch her and Victor glide around the dance floor, their feet barely touching the ground.

I place the cup of tea in her good hand. "There you go, Mother."

She tries to take a sip. I sit opposite. There's not much furniture apart from a small table with a framed photo on it. The photo is angled so it can be seen from the bed. The floor space is taken up with the hoist, lumber roll, blue plastic body pillow and other paraphernalia.

The cup lists in Mother's hand.

"Watch out," I shout. Some tea sloshes out over the side of the cup.

"I'm such a messer." As she attempts to smile, immutable pain is engraved on her face.

Next time she manages to take a drink without spilling the tea. Usually it falls on the floor in a puddle. If we use a straw, it trembles towards her lips, then tips out of the cup and lands in her lap. A beaker is easier for her to manage, but she doesn't like the taste of the plastic. She clasps the white cup with both hands now, hands I remember from childhood. I used to marvel at her painted nails, longing to become a woman like her. I remember those hands brushing my hair, turning the pages of bedtime books, comforting me. Now I brush her sparse hair, read to her, comfort her.

"Want one of these?" I show Mother the catering pack of digestive biscuits that she can't open herself.

She shakes her head, then jiggles her left hand before attempting another sip. A metallic Medic-Alert bracelet dangles on her wrist since her stint in Intensive Care with anaphylactic shock. She is allergic to penicillin.

Even the smallest dose could be fatal.

It's easy to order penicillin online without a prescription.

I have a supply at home. It stays in date for three years.

In bed at night, I fantasise about helping Mother to die.

I couldn't cope without Kate and Caroline. Like Mother, they get rashes from make-up and jewellery as well as asthma attacks, hay fever and insect bites.

"What day is it today, Deirdre?"

"Friday, Mother."

She asks the same things every day. I pour more tea. Realising how hungry I am, I reach for a biscuit and hear her say: "I wish I was dead."

"I know you do, but it's not easy to die."

"What age am I?"

"Seventy nine."

"Am I really? What day is it today, Deirdre?"

"Still Friday."

She manages a faint smile.

I help her with her tea. The pain from her many ailments, fractured spine and pressure sores is obvious. She can barely talk.

"It's my back." She tries to move. Unable to adjust her body, there is no relief. "I can't bear it, Deirdre." I go and search for a staff member.

***

Two weeks later she takes a sudden turn. A cardiac event, the doctor says. It would be cruel to send her to hospital, he tells us. She is really dying this time. For the next while she lies in bed, too ill to be hoisted out. She keeps asking for "the tablet'. The three of us have taken leave from work. For the few days one of us has stayed with her day and night. As soon as we get our families sorted, we come in. It's easier than fretting at home.

Mother drifts into a kind of sleep. "Let's get a coffee from the kitchen while she's asleep and have it in the library," Kate says. The library is a room at the end of the corridor that's usually empty, with big armchairs, a coffee table, bookshelves and a desk with a computer. The odd time you might see a resident talking to a family member on Skype.

Kate places her coffee on the little table. "The palliative team can't do any more. I was on to them again. You'd think in this day and age –"

"I'm bringing the penicillin in with me in the morning," I inform my sisters.

None of us speak for a while.

"There'll be a post mortem," Caroline says, breaking the silence. "You'll go to jail. Jenny's only fourteen.." She gets up and goes over to the door. "Will I close it?"

"No," I say. "They like it propped open like that." One of the care assistants goes past wheeling Mrs Norris and waves in.

"Would you be doing it for her or for you?" Caroline asks as she sits down again.

"I'm sick of beating myself up."

"What if it doesn't work? What if she ends up worse?"

"It will work."

Caroline massages her temples. "It would be murder."

"Well, it shouldn't be. Helping a loved one to die shouldn't make you a criminal." I take a sip of coffee, too stressed to let my anger surface.

"You'll go to jail," Caroline says. "Lose your job – be locked away from Jenny, Donal, everyone." Kate nods in agreement.

"Do you think I don't know that? You two don't have – "

Kate stands up. "We'd better go back. Don't do anything till we are all here."

"I'm staying the night," Caroline says.

***

"How are things?" I ask the next morning.

"Terrible," Caroline says. "If I'd had the penicillin last night, I'd gladly have given it to her."

Kate arrives. Mother's distress is obvious. Caroline closes the door. It doesn't lock, for health and safety reasons. We sit in silence around the bed, frozen with apprehension. Mother looks tiny. Her legs lie bent underneath the white sheet as though half of her is missing. We have a small window of opportunity to give her "the last supper" before the staff come in to turn her.

From my handbag I pull out the zip-lock bag filled with yellow-and-red capsules. Mother is upright, her hands resting on the steel safety bars. She watches Kate empty the powder from about twelve capsules into the beaker and stir in some water. She was never religious, so we don't say prayers. Spirituality was a crutch that gave way a long time ago so why introduce it now? Instead, we prattle on about this and that. Caroline holds her hand.

37

"Remember when you got the cannabis, thinking it would help the MS?" she says. "You hid the tinfoil packages in your Oxo cubes, remember? And the driving lessons with the hand-controlled car. What was that driving school called again?"

"Round the Bend," says Kate, from the opposite side of the bed. "The day your motorized wheelchair was stolen," she adds, "that was the worst'.

I join in. "And the way the four of us would dance around the kitchen when we all lived at home." I stand up and dance with an imaginary partner in the narrow space between the table and the wall. "Slow slow, quick quick, slow. Slow slow, quick – "

The framed photo crashes to the floor, jolting us back to the task in hand. Kate hands the drink to me. The enormity of what we are doing is reduced to a plastic beaker.

"That should do it," Kate says. Watched by Mother, she hurriedly gathers up the discarded shells and unused capsules and shoves them in her bag. When I ask Caroline to guard the door, I see the fear in her eyes. Mother is conscious. What if I mess up? I block out misgivings by fixing my mind on what I have to do. I hold the beaker towards Mother's pursed lips. Beneath her agony, I sense a layer of relief.

The beaker trembles in my clammy hand. She forces her head towards the drink.

"Under the bed," she says. We look at one another and shrug.

She whispers, "Always my best girls." I gently pour the liquid into her mouth. She manages to swallow it, pauses, opens her mouth for more, then bravely gulps the rest. She lies back and closes her eyes. Her face turns red, then ivory. Her breath seems to come from her throat, then stops.

The beaker feels like a grenade. Better rinse it out. On my way to the bathroom, I peep under the bed. Wow. A dropped yellow-and-red capsule glints up at me.

***

Laid out in her room, Mother lies still like a beautiful doll. Her olive green dress is missing a button. It is so strange to see her legs straight. They had to break them. We stay with her for ages. I expect her to respond when I kiss her forehead, to ask how old she is, what day it is today.

We make our way out to the car park. It is an ordinary day for everyone else. The pathway is strewn with brittle leaves that once clothed the trees. A single golden leaf floats to the ground.

Tannith Perry
England

3rd Prize
Short Story

One Complete Moment

Beyond the door are horrors. But they can be avoided most days and inside I have everything I need. Today, for a treat, I have set the table for afternoon tea with my great-great-grandmother's hand painted china. Cups as delicate as a puff of summer air. I never get tired of holding them up to the light to see the faint blue violets and trailing green vines. There are matching saucers and even two real silver spoons, which simply by sitting in your hand convey an elegant preponderance. To complete the illusion I slide the heavy satin curtains closed to block the ugliness outside the window and twist the little nub switches on the lamps. I prefer candle but the matches are getting low. The only thing missing is a lovely warm fire, but such luxuries have long been impossible. Though a while back I did manage to locate an old-fashioned wood burning oven. I cut out a picture of a fire from a magazine and pasted it inside its window. Now when the candles are lit, it looks nearly real. Or maybe it doesn't, but I've become skilled at pretending.

Once I've had my tea I turn my focus to my collection of books and art. First, on go the little cotton gloves with the fiddly buttons at the wrist. I have a special apparatus for fastening those. You won't want to ask how much that cost. I own 398 books, as well as oil paintings, pencil sketches, maps of countries which don't exist anymore, glass bottles in the colours and designs of the past, a few rocks with impressed fossils and even a piece of coral. At one point my friend Marcel said to me, "It is more reasonable to devote one's life to women (he meant men in my case) than to postage stamps, old snuff-boxes, or even to paintings and statues." I think about this admonishment sometimes while I dust my treasures but console myself with the thought that if he'd lived to see the present age he'd most likely feel

41

differently.

Not that I haven't experienced my share of men. I spent most weekends dancing in dim halls and converted cafes, after all. And my husband— kind, quiet Christopher— kept me company through the war. But then like so many others he succumbed to the illness, the name of which no one likes to say aloud; as if by whispering it you'll wake the bacteria from its slumber and tempt it to go tearing through the streets once more. Despite taking care of him when the hospital was too full to take any more patients, I never got ill, from it or any other superbug. I've thought many times how much easier it would have been just to curl up beside him on the blood flecked sheets and give into it. But somehow, for some reason, I didn't.

Enough.

Such a dark mood calls for the incomparable light of Italy. I know a room with a view, in a little hotel with painted ceilings and red tile floors, overlooking the Arno. Of course, I also know the people well who gather there and would benefit from their company. But then the bell tinkles.

My heart genuflects and I stand, hand at my throat for several seconds. With all my being I want to ignore it. I could ignore it. I have ignored it before. But there are always consequences.

I pick up my cashmere shawl, wrap it around my shoulders tightly and tiptoe to the door. I know I am being ridiculous. Do not mistake otherwise. But I can't help it.

The screen on the back of the door is flashing with menace. With a trembling finger I reach towards NEW MESSAGE.

THIS APARTMENT IS SCHEDULED FOR DEMOLITION AS PER CITY ORDINANCE 9.875. YOU HAVE THIRTY DAYS TO VACATE THE PREMISES. PLEASE SIGN TO ACKNOWLEDGE RECEIPT.

I close my eyes. I see the lawn of my childhood, the purple shadows slowly, quietly lengthening. Women in large hats chatting languidly in whicker chairs, cigarettes forgotten in lazy hands, dangling. Books, real books, strewn about the grass.The peace and elegance of such a scene holds me safe for a moment. But then I open my eyes and try to imagine what I will do. No, I cannot. It's too much.

***

I chose this building twenty years ago because it was the oldest inside

42

and out, that I could afford. Architects or builders or whoever decided such things, seemed happy to leave the exterior of older buildings alone but the insides were stripped out and modernised. Maybe it isn't their fault, maybe it is merely market forces. Nearly everything bad is. The populace demands smart homes with all the latest capabilities and compatibilities. I've learned some of the lingo but I have little idea what it means. My nephew tried to explain it to me when we were looking at apartments years ago. "It means your phone can talk to your central home control and your central home control can talk to your sound system and your refrigerator and all your other appliances." He said this like it was a good thing. But all I could think of was the horrible buzzing noise of all those machines speaking to each other.

Even this apartment has more technology then I am completely comfortable with. But I have to be honest, there are benefits. A long while back my nephew set up my fridge to order my groceries automatically. Based on how much and what I ate, my groceries would show up every seven to ten days without me having to go outside or crack open my ageing computer. This is a blessing.

Though the delivery still has to be received.

This evening there are two of them; teenagers with strange hair and those face tattoos that blink on and off. "Would you like us to bring your food inside?" one says.

I hate having strangers come in but the truth is that lifting bags is getting harder and harder, so I nod. The other one lifts the plastic crate and carries it inside, banging the moulding around the door as he does. I wince but say nothing. What's the point?

They have to pass through the living room before they can set the food on the kitchen table and they stop and stare.

"Woah! Kenson, check out this place"

"It's like a museum."

"You can leave it on the table," I say.

"Sure. Shirt. Shiriamo," says the first one. I have no idea what this means but he doesn't seem put off by my tone. Which further confirms my theory that these days you practically have to shout at someone to get them to understand you are bothered. A mere tone or rigid facial expression no longer communicates anything.

"Aren't you worried about being burnt to gobbets? I mean serious fire hazard, right?"

I just stare at the boy. Straight in the eyes and say nothing. It's my weapon of last resort. This boy lasts only two seconds before turning and scuttling back towards the front door.

"You still need to sign," says the other one. He is braver. He stares back and proffers me the little grey box. I push my thumb into it and twist, just as my nephew had taught me. But of course it won't imprint. It takes five tries to get it right. All the meanwhile, the boy is coaching me—this boy who's probably never read a whole book in his life, who probably thinks Addis Ababa is a shoe brand— speaking to me like I am mentally incapacitated.

I shut the door with a groan and drop back into my armchair. I am safe. For another seven to ten days.

I used to have visitors, but once you get to my age your friends start dropping like flies. It got so every week I'd hear of another one, in the newspaper, on the television, by telephone. I still remember the time I'd planned lunch for my actor friend Paul Lanning only to receive a phone call ten minutes before he was scheduled to arrive saying he'd bit the bullet a few hours before. After that I stopped inviting people over and decreased my interaction with the outside world.

That is the beauty of book friends. They never die, and as long as you don't drop them in the bath too many times, they don't desert you.

***

By the following morning the flashing of the doorscreen has gained a new urgency. It has gone from green to blood red and there is now a beeping. It comes at ten minute intervals and lasts for three minutes. I time it using the pocket watch I keep in the pocket of my silk smoking jacket. Not that there is any use in me knowing this. It is useless information, but if you believe Shakespeare, "Ignorance is the curse of God; knowledge is the wing wherewith we fly to heaven." Though how this information will help me fly to heaven is currently beyond me.

The last time I went outside was when my telephone stopped working and I was ill. It was only a chest infection but the rattling when I breathed was starting to scare me so out I went to face the world. For something so simple I wasn't given a real doctor of course. Just a trained technician with a white coat that didn't hide his mesh pink shirt underneath.

"If you'll just lift your arms so I can scan you," he said, then waved the hand held box, the replacement doctor they were calling it, over my body. Next I was left alone in a room while a computer asked me questions. At the end it printed out my diagnosis on a little piece of paper: Acute bronchitis.

"I could have told you that," I said to the empty room.

This morning I am just dipping my knife into my homemade bilberry jam when I hear a tapping on the living room window. As my apartment is on the third floor, this is incredibly alarming. I go to the window and pull back the curtain, bracing myself for the ugly modern buildings across the way. There is some kind of a drone attached with four suckered feet to the glass and it is projecting text onto the window. I scan it quickly. More of the same, but now with implied threats. Building to be demolished. You must get out. Or else.

The beeping of the screen, which has increased to five minute intervals and the knocking of the drone, which does not pause, is starting to get to me. They have found the only commodities I value: quiet and peace of mind.

After three days I give in and push my thumb into the doorscreen where directed. The beeping stops and blessed silence once more returns. However, a countdown now appears: 10 days, 12 hours and 42, no 41 seconds left until I must be out.

Now that I've been invaded and threatened by both the screen and a drone, I decide I need to make up my mind and to do that I must leave the flat.

The elevator requires the usual thumb signature and I can't face messing about with it, so I take the stairs, hanging onto the bannister with both hands. Bump bumping down, trying not to remember how I used to dance, my feet flashing so quickly I swear they blurred.

Then outside.

It doesn't seem possible for the air to have changed in the last thirty years but gradually it has. It now tastes sanitised. Maybe it's the way the new chemicals smell or the fact that most of the rainforest is gone as well as the majority of the Earth's true wilderness or maybe it's the city itself that taints the air. All the digitised, neon, LED lights and the solar panels, glass and metal so cold and burnished, stripping the wind of anything biological. But I seem to be the only one who notices anything amiss. People walk past my building intent and serious. My apartment is, after all, close to the financial district.

I walk to the taxi stand and wait in a short line. I decide to visit

Greenbank, the artsy neighbourhood I used to live in when Christopher was alive. Of course it will have changed but they cannot have stripped away all of the beauty. I tell the taxi to go slowly and after a second the screen in the backseat says, 'Command Engaged,' and we creep along the street. I crane my head to look up out the window; there are still many familiar buildings in graceful brick, even a few with art deco flourishes. It's the people who have changed; no one is scruffy, wearing thrift store clothing or carrying an instrument case. They all look as if they've been inside a stone polisher and come out perfect, smooth and shiny. Then in the centre of Greer park I see a hologram sculpture. I tell the taxi to pull over and wait. I get out to take a closer look. It begins as a small sapling pushing its way up to the sky. It continues to grow into a youthful tree branching out and unfurling its leaves while wind comes to harry it, snow accumulates and rain prickles its delicate bark. It is realistic and yet somehow unlike any tree I've ever seen in real life. It is beautiful. And as I watch I feel all the fears crowding around inside me subside and there is a clear, clean space. I breathe. The leaves start to ripen and grow bright with pigment, then fall. A red one drifts down near me and I watch its path with something like affection. It lands at my feet and I read: Mulcathy Life Insurance: Make the End of Life as Beautiful as the Start.

I turn back to the taxi, slamming the door harder than I need to. "Take me to the Yodale Cafe Drive through."

"Command Engaged," the screen says.

In the drive through a human voice comes out of the speaker. "What can I get for you?"

"A jasmine tea, please," I say.

"I'm sorry but we no longer sell tea."

"No tea of any kind?"

"Sorry, no. But we do have a new warm beverage called Jimador, which is proving very popular. Would you like to try one?"

"No." Despite my urge to rail, I force myself to be polite. "Thank you."

After the car passes through the drive-in, I start to cry. Actually cry.

Once again I have to be begrudgingly thankful for technological advances, because if a human had been driving, this would have been incredibly embarrassing. As we pull up to my apartment, the car's only comment on my pathetic behaviour is, "Your account has been debited

$800. Thank you for riding with us."

If I wanted to cry there were plenty of reasons to do so, the sea recently claiming back huge swaths of the poorest parts of Asia, was just one of many very understandable impetuses. But no, I am crying because a cafe no longer serves tea.

After that the decision is simple.

The screen reads 09 days 16 hours and 45 minutes. I spend a good portion of those nine days with my friends, wandering the halls of Pemberly and Brideshead Castle, being a tourist with Isabel Archer and Lucy Honeychurch and listening in on the thoughts of Henry Scobie (If one knew, he wondered, the facts, would one have to feel pity even for the planets? If one reached what they called the heart of the matter?"). I only have time to dip in to my favourite bits and then out come the scissors.

I cut into each volume, trying to maintain the integrity of each page and slice cleanly at the margin, near the spine. Little white gloves be damned, I smooth the old pages with my palms, closing my eyes to better feel the texture. I imagine the words lifting their backs like cats to get the full effect of my stroke. And just like cats I murmur to them as I work, reassuring them that I mean no harm. Some of the pages I fold, others I leave flat. But the effort of cutting, stroking and folding, or not folding, every single page of 398 books cannot be underestimated. My hands cramp and I have to stop often for breaks. I drink tea with wild abandon and play my record player as loud as I like, even through the night. The truth is I am having the best time I've had in a long time.

When the books are done I start in on the paintings, maps and drawings. This is a much more delicate operations. Over each piece I have to decide whether simply to remove it from its frame and leave it whole or cut it into smaller sections. In the end I cannot bear to maim the oils but take great pleasure is dividing the nudes into squares. When skilfully rendered, the human body looks beautiful even in small glimpses.

When the countdown clock reads: 1 day, two hours and 14 minutes I gather up my cleaved treasures and pile them near the window.

I wait until rush hour and then drop the book pages, sections of map and pieces of art out the window in large armfuls, laughing as they flutter down like a massive flock of birds. So many heads turn to look up, startled into forgetting their phone or 3D overlay. Surprise, wonder, confusion... I see so many variations of these expressions and also arms, reaching up to grab a piece. It is a beautiful spectacle. I laugh again and clap with the pure, complete joy of it. And that is what I think of later when the end comes: all those faces reaching to pluck a shard of beauty from the sky.

Hazel Atkinson
Scotland
Highly Commended
Short Story

Barbed Wire

It is raining. Water spills from an iron sky, flooding the gutters and rushing down the street in long, mud-churned funnels. Trees groan under the weight, their wood swelling bloated and dark as they try to shake it from their limbs, while drains belch, overflowing.

The lamb is trapped. It is looking up at him, pathetic - shaking, shaking and of course that's making matters worse as cruel barbs hook into its young body and it slips and slides on unsteady feet. Bleat, bleat. Where's its bloody mother? Probably down there, with the rest of the flock. They'd watched him as he staggered past, eyes bright in their placid, rain-soaked faces. Refused to move from beneath the old oak. *You'll regret that if it turns to thunder!* he snarled, savage, and they'd backed further under its branches. Bugger them. And bugger this one as well, stupid creature not to follow the rest down the hill, look where that had got it: hanging limp like dirty washing. He glares down and it whimpers back, eyes black with terror. He has seen eyes like that before. *Bugger it.*

***

He slams the kitchen door as he enters and stands for few moments on the brown mat, dripping. Wipes his dirt-caked boots but does not bother to remove them as he crosses to the fire, leaving a trail of dark footprints. Helen frowns.

There's blood, on your hands. Her eyes fixed firmly on her knitting: *click-clack* it flies beneath small fingers, *click-clack.*

He looks at her, incredulous. Does she think he hasn't noticed? *Lamb got caught on wire. Whole field's a quagmire.*

So I see. Keeping her voice very even.

What's that supposed to mean?

Nothing dear, I just meant –gesturing –*your boots, the mud* –

51

His face blackens. *Christ's sakes woman, can a man not catch his breath for a minute without being hounded in his own home?*
I didn't mean –
I know fine well what you meant. He glowers, but bends down all the same to pull off the offending footwear and damp socks. His skin shines, pale and naked; blue veins bulging across thin bones. He flinches slightly as the heat from the flames strokes feeling back into them. *Happy now?*
Helen's jaw twitches, but her fingers do not wobble: *click-clack.*
I said, are you happy now?
Don't look up. *Yes, thank you love. You'll be wanting your tea?*
He grunts, flexes long toes.
Just as you please. She places her knitting down carefully, mid-row. *It's still hot.*
Helen moves quietly across the cold flagstones, her strong, capable body held taught with learned concentration. Slow, measured movements as she pours the thick broth. He slides on the old pair of slippers she has placed to warm by the grate and unscrews the cap of a half-empty bottle of whisky, pouring himself a large dram that he swallows in one. Helen's teeth start to tingle, but he just screws the bottle shut once more and throws himself into a chair. Little breaths run through her. She wants to ask him to wash his hands; she can see the rust-like stains lining the grooves of his palms, his nails, but then she notices the look on his face and keeps her mouth shut.
Here you are, there's bread to go with it as well.
He makes an unintelligible sound as she places the dish in front of him, before falling upon it like a man half-starved, pausing only to wipe his mouth on the sleeve of his shirt. She watches him, judging the moment. Pulls at the knots in her swollen thumb.
John? Her voice is mild. *Was the lamb alright?*
He stills for a moment, hunk of bread halfway to his mouth. Then, shrugging – *Who knows.*

***

It is raining again, but harder, heavier rain that smacks off tin helmets creating a rat-a-tat-tat orchestra quickly drowned out by the whistles and white sound of shells and bullets; the mud rising above his knees as he tries to push forward but stumbles again and again palms outstretched Wait! he calls to the shadowy figure ahead and Stop! Stop!

Wait for me! it does not listen and he is seized with a sudden knowledge that something terrible is about to happen the oh God oh God please no spinning useless around his head Stop stop! Where are you? lunging forward as the earth explodes beneath him; crawling spitting dirt blinded by smoke and debris and deafened by noise to new dumb silence until his nose smacks straight into something warm and he knows without real knowing that he has found him; slow dread creeping through his veins and looking up oh God oh God no the young man hangs there and he is Jesus On The Cross with barbed-wire holding him up like some perverse scarecrow while scarlet blood so bright! on this khaki unreal landscape pumps from his neck his head his holy hands in sickening bursts oh god oh please please no; dead eyes are liquid ink screaming star-like at him as he stands there unable to move to speak to think to pray and then suddenly they are the lamb's eyes it is the lamb's small white body hung from iron thorns like a sacrifice as oh God no it shrieks its agony –

***

He jolts awake, stars exploding behind his own lids as he rubs a fist across, feels the mud and blood drain slowly from them. Quiet, quiet he tells himself; he can still hear that agonized cry in his ears but he knows this too will soon fade. Except, this time, it doesn't. He strains for a moment, listening. Faint, but unmistakable; a thin wail from somewhere outside the sturdy stone walls.

Helen – he nudges her *–Helen, do you hear that?*

Hmm? She is drowsy, heavy-lidded. *Charlie?*

His chest tightens. Nausea pulls and aches his stomach down, tugs lead-like at his gut; his heart jumps and frets and he stares at her. Her mouth works beside him for a few moments before widening slack with the deep, even breaths of sleep. Quietly, carefully he edges from the bed. The floor is cold on his bare feet as he creeps from the room and down, down the stairs while wind rattles angrily at the windows he passes, thin branches scratching along in mimicry of sharp talons. Stupid, he thinks, probably just the gale you can hear. Go back to bed. And yet – still that sound, someway above the noise of the storm; that awful, endless wail and getting nearer, or so it seems. He reaches the fireplace. There are still embers burning and the faint, orange glow and comforting warmth draws him like a moth as he crouches, whisky bottle clutched between his two hands. His fingers shake a little as he gulps,

53

his wife's sleepy murmur: *Charlie?* like a boxer's blow. He tips the bottle up again, stares into the coals.

There – again. No mistaking it this time, a howling curse way above the wind. Black eyes, barbed wire: *leave me* he thinks. Hugs the whisky to him like a charm. Moaning right outside now: is he being visited by some Dickensian spirit? *Just stories, children's stories.* Will Marley clank through the letter box and wrap heavy chains around his neck? *Leave me, leave me.* He knows it won't. Lurches to the door and heaves it open to meet his tormentor.

There, on the doorstep, is the lamb.

His breathing slows; he sways a little. It looks at him. Bleat, bleat. Straight from the Book of Revelation, he thinks, something of the lion in this one. Bleat, bleat. Coat matted and spattered thick with blood and grime. Bleat, bleat. Would it have knocked, if it could?

What do you want? Hadn't meant to whisper. Words whipped away.

Bleat, bleat. Water rising around its wobbling legs.

You can't come in.

Bleat, bleat. One ragged ear where the wire has torn it, shivering now. Those eyes.

Bugger you.

A small bundle – wrapped up in a dry towel it looks like a new-born, cradled in his arms. He remembers the day they brought Helen back from the hospital with a bundle like that; his quiet joy and her still weak from a long labour but smiling up at him, beautiful.

Stupid boy he says, softly *Going where you oughtn't. Where you've no business being.* He runs a thumb along its raw and jagged ear, clean now and crusting over. The lamb wriggles, but does not cry out. He takes another gulp of whisky. *So, Revelation begins at my back door does it? Come to forgive my sins?*

It blinks up at him. Long, dark lashes. An innocent face.

No need to hang yourself up for me. My wife believes I'm doing a good job all by myself. He pauses, takes another swig. Clear amber now, he can see the bottom of the bottle each time he raises it.

I heard her. He informs the lamb. *She doesn't know, but* I heard *her.* Helen had accepted his defection from the Church to a Sunday morning working the fields with good grace and without question. Perhaps she had thought to pray for both of them. Perhaps she'd thought he wouldn't notice that she stayed longer and longer after the service each week. But of course, he had.

I thought she might be leaving me. For someone more holy, a man of God. You understand?

The lamb looks sceptical.

So I followed her.

The smooth wood caressing his ear, brown and burnished. Sound travelling through as he'd leaned against it. First, the soft drawl of the pastor: *Helen, what is it, do you think, that your husband means to achieve through this behaviour?*

Reverend. His wife's voice had sounded choked. *I do believe he's* crucifying *himself.*

And he had seen sharp wire tearing soft flesh, and felt sick.

The lamb bleats softly and he shushes it, puts a big finger to its mouth. It latches on, suckling; it is hungry. He reaches over.

Here. Bottle-feeding, he thinks as the little creature slurps at the warm milk he produces, we'll never get rid of it now. I'm going soft.

***

No bottles. Helen had said, firmly. *I'm going to feed him myself. To make him strong, like me.*

And she had. That amazed him as well, how that small bundle had swelled, *thrived* on nothing but milk as if it were no more than a kid, or calf. Amazed him too when he began crawling around the wooden furniture; running and tumbling through the muddy yard on fat legs; begging for a pet (a chick, a pony, anything!) for his own. His mother smiled, indulged him, then put her foot down. He looks down at his own feet, dry and smooth now. Skin turned sponge-like when it was damp for too long, became waterlogged. Saturated. Toes grew pale and porous and distant from the rest of the body; just dead, bloated creatures. He wiggles and feels warm life run through them.

Stern, strong Helen. His farm, but things were run her way: her bread, her butter, her eggs she'd boast happily. An iron fist and velvet glove all in one as she swatted at them with her broom *out! Out my kitchen both of you you're filthy!* before humming things happily back into order while they giggled, guilty. *My goodness* as she hid a smile *what will I do with you?*

He remembered her outrage and frustration when both her husband and son had marched through the door to inform her that they'd enlisted and would be off to fight for King and country within the week.

No. She had said, pointing a Kitchener finger at him: you! *No, John. There's no call for you to go as well – you heard what they said, reserved occupation. That's you! We need you here on the farm, who will run things if you're gone?*

He'd just smiled, and kissed her on the forehead. *You will. Far better at it than me anyway. Besides, be home before you know it, won't we Charlie?*

Their son beamed, patriotic fervour flushing his round cheeks like communion wine. *We will. We have to support our country, our brothers!*

Helen had wept. *John, please. He's sixteen! Tell him to stay.*

He's sixteen. I can't tell a man what to do. You should be proud!

Helen's mouth set.

We'll be back soon Mam, like Dad said. And their son had kissed her on the cheek, dimpling. Even she had smiled then; he could charm the birds from the trees, everyone said. It might have been true.

***

He wonders if that was the last time he saw her smile. Better to remember that than the way her face had cracked in half when he brought home that small bundle of clothes and keepsakes. How she whispered his name just once like something very precious had been broken beyond repair. The way she'd looked at him as he lied about the swift bullet, the hero's death, hating him for it almost as much as he hated himself. He glugs down the last of the whisky, wipes numbly at wet cheeks. The lamb butts its soft chin against his own, scrapes his skin with a small, rough tongue. Bleat, bleat. His mouth twitches.

***

Helen wakes to a cold, empty bed. She frowns, wondering if she has overslept but no, the clock on the bedside table tells her it's before six. Wrapping a dressing gown about her, she treads silently down the stairs and pushes open the door.

For a moment, she cannot breathe. She looks down at the tableau before her; the blood stains on the grey floor by John's still head, the empty whisky bottle, the lifeless pile of rags. Dear God, she thinks, not while I was sleeping. Not like this alone with our cold stone beneath and me just here to clean up the mess of you. Clutching at the brass handle. And then he gives a small groan and opens his eyes, sees her standing over him, face a shadow.

He struggles to his feet, coughing; runs a hand through unkempt hair. He feels awkward, child-like almost – caught out with his blood-shot eyes and still in bed-clothes coated with black coal-dust. He holds up the towel.

Lamb came round back last night. Thought I'd better clean it up.

Helen is silent.

The lamb wriggles: bleat, bleat.

He looks at her, his wife; her proud back, her watchful gaze. He doesn't know what to say: I'm sorry? I tried? I never meant to crucify you too. Too small a sentiment, those little syllables. Instead, he clears his throat.

I'm off up field. Going to try and measure the damage. Look after –he stops *–I mean, would you please look after this one, 'til I get back. Bit more warm milk and should be right as rain.*

Helen looks down at the swaddled animal. He notices a muscle jumping in her cheek and wonders whether she is seeing what he sees. Don't say his name again, not yet and not today, he begs silently. Her eyes glitter; for a moment he wonders if she will refuse. Then -

Give him here.

***

Helen watches from the window as her husband marches up the hill, great over-coat covering his pyjamas. Something lighter in his step today? or perhaps she is imagining things, looking too greenly for any sign he might wrench the nails out. She picks up the empty bottle of whisky, wrinkling her nose and, on impulse, dashes it against the stone floor. The noise splinters through her and the lamb bleats, baleful. She looks down; sharp diamonds glint back. Then she sighs and, tucking the animal under one arm, reaches for the broom.

Margot Ogilvie
Australia

Highly Commended
Short Story

Somebody's Angel

Tiredness swept through me like a diligent maid searching for a lost jewel, stirring up dust in every corner, making the search harder. Like the fog in my brain made everything harder.

I should have been asleep.

The strange bed, the noisy room, and the twenty-four-hour comings and goings of the neonatal intensive care unit across the corridor joined forces against sleep. And they were winning.

I needed to get out of the unit for a while. My precious Michaela was sleeping soundly. I wouldn't be gone long.

My IV stand tagged along like a conjoined twin as I wandered the corridors, going nowhere in particular, yet drawn onwards by an invisible something.

I took a turn. A huge window at the end of the walkway beckoned me. The labyrinth of corridors bamboozled my inner compass and left me with no clue as to what view the furniture saw as it gazed out of the expanse of glass.

I didn't see her until my hand brushed the back of the lounge on which she sat, staring out at the lights of the city. Even if I hadn't been distracted by steering issues with the IV stand, I wouldn't have seen her. She was too short to be seen from behind.

And yet there she sat. This tiny girl. Surely no more than two-years-old. When she spotted me, she stretched one hand out to point to the lights, the city on display like the stars in the heavens.

"Pwiddy tars," she whispered, then proceeded to softly serenade the scene.

"Twingle, twingle, widdle tars…"

She either couldn't remember any more, or didn't know the rest. My inner compass couldn't resist the magnet of her smile as she patted the seat beside her. I sat, and was quickly engulfed by hands, elbows, and legs as the tiny body clambered into my barely formed lap. One arm was wrapped in a plaster cast.

"What's your name. honey?" I said quietly.

She shrugged.

I had seen no-one along the way, and, apart from a rather bedraggled teddy, we were alone.

The nymph was soon entwined around me. In no more than a dozen breaths, she was asleep.

It would have been so easy to join her, lulled by the rhythmic breathing of her sleep in this quiet corner of the hospital. It felt good, being her pillow, sensing her comfort and trust.

But no. Someone would be frantic at her loss, this treasure, this beauty.

Even her slight weight was surely over my post-op limit, but I couldn't just leave her there. She stirred slightly when I stood, only to burrow closer, her pink too-big-pyjama-clad arms clinging around my neck.

Juggling her, the teddy bear and the wayward IV stand made for slow progress. A nurse looked up as we approached the paediatric ward.

"Have you lost a broken angel by any chance?" I whispered.

"Not that I realised, but, yes, apparently we had. Thanks for returning her." Once she was successfully snuggled into her bed, with teddy safely under her arm, we slipped out into the corridor.

I wasn't expecting an explanation, although I was curious as to how a tiny child could be allowed to wander darkened hospital corridors in the middle of the night.

"It's a sad story really," the nurse said. "She has no-one except that old bear of hers."

"She's an orphan?"

"Well, yes. I can't tell you the details. Confidentiality, you know."

"Would it be all right for me to visit her, maybe tomorrow… I mean later today."

Having established permission, I headed back to the neonatal unit. I had my own angel to watch over. But somehow, I couldn't get this one out of my mind. She was nobody's angel.

***

My doctors gave me a good report later in the morning. And

60

Michaela, now ten days old, was progressing well according to her specialists. I expected nothing less. After all, she was our miracle baby. The baby they'd told me I'd never have. The baby I very nearly didn't have, until finally, after miscarriages had stolen the potential of my womb again and again, I had borne a living child. Way too early, but alive.

A hospital bed had been my prison for two months before Michaela was born. No wandering the corridors then. The time I served had great rewards, and the pregnancy lasted longer than any of my others. I made it to 32 weeks and went into early labour, again. Marcus was called in from our farm an hour and a half away, and they let labour progress.

The long road to motherhood had me looking forward to labour. To finally bringing our child into the world and becoming a family. I was, however, robbed of even that. A massive haemorrhage triggered a panic ending in the operating theatre. My hopes for more children ended there as well.

But we had Michaela, and Marcus convinced me that was enough. I was too overwhelmed by all that had happened, and was still happening, to not believe him.

I was ready for home, they told me, once the drip came out today. No way was I going home. Not without Michaela. Home was ninety minutes away. I don't know how Marcus did it, running the farm, coming in every other day to see us, being so far from Michaela.

The discharge co-ordinator said there was somewhere nearby I could stay. There was paperwork to do, finance to sort out. I could stay a few more days if I needed to.

I needed to.

I scrubbed and gowned and went to see my daughter. Like an invisible umbilical cord, love connected us. It would soon be stretched to 'somewhere nearby', but it would continue to bind us together.

As I held her tiny hand through the portals in the humidicrib, I couldn't help thinking of other tiny hands, though huge against Michaela's. Small hands pointing to twinkling star-lights. Strong arms tight around my neck.

When nurses took Michaela for more tests, I ventured to Paediatrics to visit the broken angel. I didn't even know her name. She smiled, reached for me, pleased to see me.

"What's to become of her?" I asked the social worker who came in while I was reading her a story. She directed me to her office near the nurses' station.

"She'll be placed in another foster situation until someone expresses interest in adopting her."

"Another foster situation? What happened to the previous one?" I knew I had no right to ask, but that same something that drew me down the corridor the previous night now urged me onwards again.

"I can't really say, you know, but... well, I will say that they proved to be inappropriate as foster carers. They have since been removed from the foster system and are facing court proceedings."

I'd seen enough current affairs shows to know they probably had something to do with the broken arm. My sorrow at the tragedy this little one had suffered threatened my ability to stand. I sank into the chair the social worker offered.

Emotion churned deep within me, threatening to release words that should wait. At least until I'd talked to Marcus. This wasn't something to rush into. But the volcano erupted and the lava-words flowed out.

"I want to adopt her. My husband and I will take her."

The stunned social worker stuttered and stammered about procedure and protocol. Then she touched my hand and said quietly, "You know nothing about this child. When you hear her story, you might change your mind."

"I doubt that very much. The little I already know only makes me want to take her home and keep her safe. But tell me. Tell me her story."

The hardness that came from years working with troubled people in a troubled 'system' serving a troubled world moved over to let compassion reign as the social worker spoke.

"Jane was found abandoned, wrapped in bloodied newspaper, in a park in the inner city. Appeals on TV and social media eventually brought the mother out of hiding. She was fifteen. She'd been raped by a gang of drunks who were never caught."

I inhaled sharply. It had happened again. To someone else. The social worker went on, her words pulling me away from my thoughts.

"She was so ashamed when she found out she was pregnant, she ran away. There was no prenatal care, no hygienic delivery. Both girls had serious health issues."

Hearing her story only served to fuel my determination. It could have so easily been my story. The words penetrated the walls I had built over the years. I felt her shame as my own.

I needed to get away from here before the past I thought I had dealt with revealed itself in technicolour reruns all over this woman's sterile office. I tossed an "I'll be back later," over my shoulder as I hurried from the room to my own. A journey that would take me twenty years and back.

I was gang raped when I was fifteen. Thankfully, I didn't get pregnant, but the emotional scars it left me with had taken years to get over. Or perhaps I was still getting over it.

After five years in therapy, I finally had the courage to date. It took Marcus another five years to prize open the oyster shell of my life and expose the pearl inside. He'd seen it from the start, but knew I needed to see it too. He spent those years patiently being there for me, even when I was horrible to him. Ten years after the attack, I was ready to commit to Marcus, the man I had grown to love.

I was delighted when the loving intimacy that came with our marriage completely confirmed that my past was just that – past. Then other devastating consequences of the attack revealed themselves. My emotional scars may have healed, but physical scars lay hidden deep within, causing a cortege of miscarriages.

Surgery allowed me to carry Michaela as long as I had. Each week that I was able to mark off the calendar turned hatred to healing, and healing to hope. When she passed the critical date for survival, I thought I was again done with the past and its indignity. Until the surgery that saved my life and hers left me unable to carry life within me again. Hope turned to hurt again.

And now there was Jane – a generic name for an unwanted, unloved beauty who deserved a name of her own, and so much more.

My journey through the dark valley of memories ended at Michaela's crib, and I started telling her about her new big sister. About how they'd play together. Grow together. Laugh together. And love each other.

I phoned Marcus, and poured out my grief for the children we'd lost, my gratitude for the child I had delivered, my great desire to give Jane a real home and a real name. I wanted to do it for her, for her mother, and for me. I told him about her smile, her pink-pyjama-cuddles, her brokenness and her very sad teddy.

He fell in love with her over the phone.

Sure, there'd be paperwork, process and protocol, but in our hearts, she was ours already. The substance of our unspoken dreams.

"Let's make Jane our Joanna. It means precious gift," Marcus said before he ended the call, promising to see his three beautiful girls the next day.

Two little girls. Both precious, beautiful angels. Both priceless gifts. First Michaela, then Joanna.

First healing, now wholeness.

Nobody's angel no longer, Joanna had parents who loved her, a tiny sister to love. She had a family. We were a family.

She was somebody's angel now. And forever.

Valerie Bowes
England

Shortlist
Short Story

Rosemary For Remembrance

"You missed one."

Rosemary slammed the mug of tea down on the table. Roy ostentatiously wiped drops of liquid from his sweater and let the triumph and spite flow over his head.

"Missed one what?" As if he didn't know what she was getting at.

"A weed. What else? In the veg patch. Beside the third carrot on the right. You'd better run out and get rid of it at once, hadn't you, before it ruins the garden?"

She marched out, closing the door behind her with unnecessary venom. Roy looked in distaste at the anaemic tea that puddled the table. She knew he liked it dark and strong. And it wouldn't have enough sugar in it. It never did, these days.

He left it undrunk and wandered over to stare out of the window at the perfection beyond. What made Rosemary hate the garden so much? It wasn't as if he'd sprung it on her out of the blue. She'd known of his passion for gardening before they'd even thought of getting married.

He'd grown the flowers for her bridal bouquet. It meant so much more than a florists' creation, she said, burying her nose among the fat yellow roses and frilly pinks, and she'd looked at him with love in her eyes when she discovered the sprig of honey-scented rosemary tucked in the centre.

If he grew anything for her nowadays, it would be hemlock and poison ivy.

They'd bought this house less for the rather tatty accommodation and more for the quality of the soil in the large, overgrown garden.

"As you can see, it does need a bit of TLC," the Estate Agent said, ushering them into the sittingroom and choosing his words with care. "But it's definitely got potential. A coat or two of paint – and maybe get rid of the purple wallpaper?"

They'd all laughed.

"Consider it done!" Roy said. He wasn't bothered about the purple wallpaper, although it wouldn't have been his choice. He'd let Rosemary decide how she wanted the house. He wouldn't interfere with that, but the garden was going to be his. He couldn't wait to get started.

"It's bit big for the two of us, but it'll be great for a family," she'd said, the night they moved in. The sparsely furnished rooms had echoed softly under their feet as they walked around their new kingdom and he clamped her close to his side when they at last stood at the bedroom window.

"Just you wait and see what I can make of this garden, Rose. Give me a year or two and you won't recognise it. Flower beds around a central lawn. Veggie patch over there, where the light's best. Fruit bushes there, and I might even see if an apricot would grow against that wall. Apples and pears too – you can get lovely dwarf stock varieties that wouldn't take up too much room. Or how would you like a cherry? Have to net it from the birds, mind, but that's no problem. Fresh fruit and veg, love! Ours will be the best-fed kids anywhere."

He'd always assumed that children would be part of his life. Like seedlings. He'd already mentally portioned out little patches for them, so they could begin to learn the art of gardening. But Rosemary's resentment of the love and care he lavished on the garden increased as the years went by and no children appeared. When the last IVF treatment failed and the last hope faded, he'd tentatively suggested adopting. She'd glared at him with something approaching hatred.

"So you want to do a graft because I'm inadequate, do you? Barren stock, don't you call it? Just because they say you're not firing blanks, it's all my fault?"

"Of course it isn't. I don't think that for a minute," he'd said. It was exactly what the doctor at the Fertility Clinic had told them, but he was only too aware of how knife-edge her temper had become. Back then, he'd still had room for sympathy. Being childless affected her more than it did him. He could accept it. She couldn't. 'It's just that – well, we've got all this room here and we could give some kid a good home.'

"You make it sound like taking on an abandoned puppy," she snapped. "Don't say things you don't mean, Roy. You, letting a child loose to play in your precious garden? Oh, yes, I can just see that happening! You'd have a heart attack every time it moved but I suppose at least it wouldn't pee on the lawn."

He'd have been all right with it then, he thought, remembering. He'd have set up a play area, a real superduper one. Climbing frames, swing, soft bark cover. These days, to be honest, Rosemary would be right.

But it was too late, anyway. Years of hope and endeavour followed by failure had corroded their relationship beyond repair. Anyone could sense the caustic atmosphere the minute they set foot in the place. An Adoption Agency worth its salt would run a mile.

Now, looking out at the immaculate lawn, the borders vibrant with flowers and the espaliered apricot glowing against the wall, he wondered for the umpteenth time why he stayed. Why he didn't just leave her.

The answer was in front of him. She'd take him for every penny she could, which would mean selling the house. He'd lose the garden into which he'd poured all the love that Rosemary didn't want any more. He couldn't bear that.

But neither could he stand this much longer. With a final glance of distaste for the pale, cold and untouched tea, he went out to his shed.

***

It must have been the cheerful whistle that made Matt Wilkins look over the fence. Normally, the neighbours weren't encouraged to peer into the garden and engage in idle chitchat. Rosemary made it clear she considered it vulgar. She didn't want to know them.

Hearing a tentative 'Good morning!' Roy stopped digging, rested his foot on his spade and returned Matt's greeting.

"Looking great!" Matt observed. "What're you planting?"

"Rosemary." Roy grinned at him. "Great with lamb. The old bush was getting very leggy, so I took some cuttings a while back. Just about ready to make it on their own now."

He picked up one of the pots and displayed it to Matt's admiring eyes.

"Cool! You've certainly got green fingers. Wish things would grow like that for me, but they just curl up and die," Matt said ruefully.

"Here, have this one. I've got more than I need." Roy went over to give it to him.

"You sure? Thanks, mate. How's the missus?" Matt felt he ought to ask, although he wasn't remotely interested in the sour-faced old boot.

"Visiting family in Australia," Roy said.

That explained the happy whistle, Matt thought, as he went indoors.

***

Roy scowled at the scatter of green shoots over the rosemary bed. He'd hoed that only two days ago. Weeds never grew that quickly in the rest of the garden. Why here? Maybe it was because it was freshly dug. Or maybe it was the manure. He decided to pull the trespassers up by hand. That way, they couldn't re-root themselves.

But the next evening, weeds were growing there again, thicker than ever. With a twinge of alarm, Roy recognised the green furled spike of couch and the heart-shaped first leaves of bindweed. What were they doing there? Getting rid of the couch grass had been a Herculean labour in the early days, but he'd done the job thoroughly. He'd never had much trouble with it since, and bindweed had never shown its face before.

He didn't want either of those in his garden. Bindweed roots, once established, went down for miles and broke as good as look at them, spawning a fresh plant with every tiny piece. So did couch, but he couldn't deep-dig this patch now. He'd lose all his newly-planted rosemary.

This was a job for a weedkiller – something he hated doing and only used when he had no other choice. He didn't want to risk spraying, so he patiently dabbed every leaf with a product that was supposed to kill only what it touched. It was almost dark when he finished and his back felt as if it was broken in half.

You'd have thought he was putting on fertiliser. The next morning, he went to check on it before leaving for the office. The green spears looked rampantly healthy and thick enough to cover the soil. Not a sign of yellowing or wilting. It'll take time to work, he told himself, but the nasty feeling in the pit of his stomach refused to go.

And he was right. The weedkiller showed no signs of working as the weeks progressed. The deep-rooted rosettes of dandelions appeared among the soaring grass, yellow flowers turning swiftly to fluffy white clocks as if they'd been fast-forwarded. Every time he went outside, seeds drifted insolently past him on their way to infest other parts of the garden.

The rosemary bed seemed to bubble weeds as a cauldron bubbles potions. No matter how hard he slaved, it was as though they spilled outwards like water, slipping through his fingers to cover the whole garden. Purple-flowered mallow snuggled close to his onions with roots that went down to Australia, and defied all attempts to pull it out without bringing up the bulb as well. Dahlias became chewed nests of earwigs, couch roots bored through his carrots and black spot appeared on the few roses that had escaped being choked to death.

Bindweed began to coil around the rosemary and ivy appeared from nowhere. Both crept over the lawn, causing the mower to stop working every five minutes as tough tendrils wound around the blades. Brown patches freckled the grass and a poisonous Giant Hogweed rocketed skywards. Roy only realised it wasn't cow parsley when it topped 6 feet high and he came out in a painful rash.

Pulling out great handfuls of grass, he felt something jab his hand and found he was grasping a stout bramble stem, bristling with thorns. Where could that have come from? They were right in the middle of suburbia. There wasn't another bramble for miles. A seed must have been dropped by a bird, he reasoned, but how had it grown this thick and vicious so quickly?

He crouched on his heels, sucking at his bleeding fingers and stared in loathing at the ground beneath the rosemary.

Going out into the garden the minute he got home, microwaving a hasty snack before working until it was too dark to see, he grew thin and grey. His colleagues at the office became increasingly concerned.

"Poor old Roy. Hasn't been the same since his wife left him," they murmured.

"Went to Australia and never came back. Ran off with a sheep farmer, so I heard."

"Oh, I thought it was India? Took up with some weird sect."

"Whatever. But he needs to pull himself together or he's heading for a break-down."

In the washroom, Roy's fingers stung as the hot water ran over them. He glared at the redness in fury. Nettles, now!

That was it. He'd had enough. Tomorrow, he'd do something about it.

For the first time he could remember, he didn't go into the garden when he got home. He bought himself a large and indulgent take-away, drew the curtains against the wilderness outside and defiantly watched television all evening with a glass of whisky in his hand.

A week later, Matt Wilkins mentioned to his wife that there was a 'For Sale' sign up next door.

"Garden's getting too much for him," he said.

***

The furniture van stood outside the gate. Roy watched as the tailgate was bolted into position.

"I'll meet you at the new place," he told the removal crew. "Just one last thing to do."

He walked through the echoing empty house and out into the garden, pushing his way through creeping masses of vegetation to where the rosemary bushes reached imploring hands skywards.

"Oh, very clever!" he said quietly. "So you thought you'd get your own back by taking my garden away from me? Well, you've done it. It's gone. I can't fight any more. I'm leaving. I've rented a little flat. Second floor, no balcony, no garden. Not even a window box. Satisfied?"

He felt a savage triumph as he got into his car. He hadn't told her about the allotment just in case, but it was far enough away to be out of reach of her creeping roots and wind-blown seeds.

She thought she'd won, but he'd fooled her.

***

It was a lovely sunny evening. The sittingroom of Roy's new flat was filled with a golden glow and the vase of sweet-peas on the table perfumed the air with their delicate scent. Plenty more where they came from, he thought, touching a rose-and-cream frilled petal with his fingertip. They'd done really well. Almost as if they were trying to make up for things.

He went out to the tiny kitchen and brought his meal back on a tray. He'd enjoy this while he watched the end of the News, and then he'd have a wander up to the allotment to do the watering and see how his runner beans were getting on. Might even be able to put some in for the Autumn Show as well as the onions. One in the eye for Rosemary, eh?

He switched on the television. They'd reached the local news section, the newscaster just coming to the end of an item.

"The remains were discovered by a landscaping contractor, called in to deal with the very over-grown garden."

A man's face filled the screen, ashen and shell-shocked.

"If it wasn't for the Lottery...We were only going to clear it up a bit, grass it over so the kids could have somewhere to play but then we won this cash and my Annie's always fancied a water feature…"

72

There was a ring at the doorbell. Roy put down his tray and went to answer it. The two men on the doorstep thrust warrant cards under his nose.

"Roy Brent? Good evening, sir. I'm Detective Inspector Miller and this is DS Hall. All right if we come in? We'd like a little chat with you. It's about your wife."

As clear as if she'd been standing beside him, Roy heard Rosemary's voice.

"Did you really think you'd won? That I'd let you forget? Let you go?"

He turned to the CID officers with a smile. "Come in. Make yourselves at home. Don't worry, I know why you're here. But before we start, just tell me this – prisons have gardens, don't they?"

Chris Connolly
Ireland

Shortlist
Short Story

The Moon is Always Escaping

I think maybe I am turning slowly insane as I grow older. An incremental degradation of my senses, what some would call my mental faculties.

Which is no surprise.

I've seen it happen enough times. Men simply snapping, literally losing their minds; and it doesn't always take much, or even very long.

I've been incarcerated since I was fifteen years old, and I am now more than twice that.

There was that spell at the beginning, a couple of years or thereabouts, when I was held in the juvenile detention centre. Before they said I was old enough to be moved to a real prison.

They called me Killer at the start. The kind of crude sarcasm you find in places like this. They'd say Killer and then laugh, because I was so young. But I'm not so young anymore, and now people mostly just call me by my name, which is Eli.

When my first parole hearing rolls around I'll be fifty. If I'm still alive, that is – and statistically speaking that is no sure thing. Even if I do reach that milestone, the chances of being granted parole, I've been told, are slim. Because of the nature of the system.

And the nature of the crime.

Though there are still appeals ongoing, even after all this time. Instigated now mainly by my father. I tolerate them only for him; the chances of my conviction being somehow overturned – after sixteen years – are not much more than nil. And hope is a very dangerous thing.

They continue to visit, my parents, nearly every single week.

It still feels strange to talk to them – by ridiculous telephone – while they sit there on the other side of that thick wire-mesh glass, just inches away. I've told them they shouldn't come so often, that it's not fair to have them make that long drive every Sunday, not fair to go through the invasive rigmarole of security screening, of needless waiting, just to speak to their orange-suited, shuffling, manacled son for an hour or two.

But they come, regardless.

Dad does most of the talking. By now I simply don't have much to say. Every day for me is a carbon copy of every other, from the time I wake to the time I eat to the time my steel cell-door slams shut and the lights go out. And even when that isn't the case, I generally hold back, because when something out of the ordinary happens here it's generally not the kind of thing you want to share with your loved ones.

My mother doesn't talk much either. Like me, I think she's all out of things to say, and so she mostly sits there and listens as my dad tries to keep the conversation moving. She doesn't let on, but I can tell she knows I won't be getting out. I think deep down my dad probably knows the same, but won't ever be able to admit it.

They are a relief though, these visits. The visiting area is a calmer space, voices soft and hushed so as not to be overheard, and the true sounds of prison life are mostly absent.

Apart from this brief respite each week, the noise in my caged world is a constant, all day and all night. Shouting, banging, cackling, clanking. Howling and weeping. Each decibel echoes against the concrete and steel, is terribly magnified. Sounds you don't want to hear, piercing your brain all twenty-four hours of the day, more than fourteen-thousand minutes of it, even in your sleep. Not to mention the smell of the place, the reek of disinfectant intermingled with the stench of hundreds of angry men living their lives in a tin bowl.

You get used to it, but you don't really.

***

I can still recall it very clearly. The incident, I mean. As if each time I close my eyes I am back there and it is happening all over again.

I can remember when it happened – after it happened – sitting in the back of a police car outside what was then my home, the entire place surrounded by flashing lights and policemen and news crews and other people, neighbours mostly, standing behind the police cordon. Just standing there, shuffling in the cold and staring, the same way people stare at car wrecks.

I can feel the handcuffs hanging loose around my wrists, shackled behind my back; can smell the dried blood all over me, that very particular metallic scent; can remember struggling to see my parents when they arrived back from work, straining over my shoulder just to catch a glimpse of them.

They looked so strange, so frantic, their faces oddly stretched and grimacing, completely confused, probably in shock.

I was in shock too, I think. I could barely speak. I could barely see through the tears. All those flashing lights and people and the police and the sheer terror. It wasn't real life, I kept telling myself. It couldn't be.

They say that the mind represses, or tries to, moments of trauma and stress. As a coping mechanism. It attempts to scour itself clean, to purge itself of the memory of turmoil and pain. Or so I've been told. But I remember it all. I wish I didn't, but it enters my mind from time to time – invades would be a better word – as if the insides of my eyelids are a cinema screen, my mind the projector, the reel stuck on repeat.

In truth this happens more than just occasionally, even after so long. And what came after – the lengthy, protracted trial, those people on the jury staring at me with eyes that from the very beginning couldn't mask their certainty of my guilt; the prosecutor, painting a picture of me as some kind of irredeemable lunatic child; the sentencing, with the judge denouncing what he described as an innate evil; and finally, the beginning of my sentence – all this I remember like it happened last week.

But after that, the sixteen years since – when I try to set it out sequentially in my mind, in detail – it seems to have vanished. I can feel it, can sense it, all that time and what it's done to me, but my mind cannot *recall* it. Not properly. I remember only little bits, slivers of snapshots.

What I remember most is the worst of it, naturally. Which was at the beginning. Oddly enough, that couple of years before I became an adult and they transferred me to a real prison with real men, hardened criminals of all ages – those first years with kids not much older than I was, and some even younger, were torture of a different kind than I have faced since.

There is something about juvenile, immature malevolence and rage which is far more intense, far more sadistic in its own way, than that of older adult men. You wouldn't think it, but it's true.

I was bullied and harassed and beaten almost every day. And worse.

You get used to it – but you don't.

77

At the time I was still coming to terms with what happened. With the murder of my little brother, Jacob. I say 'at the time', but something like that… it would take more years than we're given to truly accept or escape it.

I was just a normal teenager when it happened.

People, and the media especially, called me things like a devil-child, a miniature monster. But I loved my brother, and still do. I miss him more than I can say.

The story I told was very simple, and it never changed. I told them that I heard noises downstairs, and that when I went to investigate I found my little brother, just twelve years old, on the kitchen floor. His body odd-angled and covered in blood, the blood still warm, his body still warm but no longer breathing, the kitchen knife discarded there beside him. The back door open, the back door left ajar.

But from the get-go they seemed set on the theory that it could only have been me who carried out the act. The initial blows. And then the stabbings.

***

Time is something that no one can escape, but in here there is no hiding from it at all.

It lingers everywhere, hides behind corners and under beds, floats through walls like a cruel magic fog. The minutes can seem like hours, the hours like days, the days like years… And though I've been told that it's unhealthy to obsess over such things – over time and its ethereal elongations – that's easy to say for some state-sanctioned shrink who thinks he knows everything about everything from speaking to a few inmates for half an hour each a week. Who gets to go home to his family at the end of the day. Who can experience things like direct sunlight, or nature, or true silence, whenever he feels like it.

They call it a penitentiary, but for the average inmate penitence isn't exactly high up on their problems-to-deal-with list. Nor is it something that the system in general – from guards to wardens to politicians – seems very interested in, despite what they may publicly proclaim.

The same goes for so-called rehabilitation.

The fact is, when you put people in a cell for the bulk of their days, for years on end, they don't magically morph into upstanding and reformed citizens; when you cage someone up like an animal, an animal is usually what emerges. Like babies raised by wolves.

I know this from experience, as well as observation. I've been in solitary before, and in solitary your mind can warp. Delirium sets in. After just a few days of it even the strongest mind begins to lean towards a certain kind of psychosis.

And while hope can be a dangerous thing, time – the creeping strangeness of *time* – can be fatal.

You pace, because there's nothing else to do. You begin to talk to yourself, because there's no one else to talk to. You bang your head against the wall, because there is no other way to vent the maddening frustration and desperation instilled by sensory deprivation. And you scream and wail, because soon enough the fact of infinity becomes lodged in your consciousness, and that's all you have left.

You scream into a void. You go in there one way and you come out another, a different kind of your self with a new distorted mind.

This change can happen so easily, so quickly... but changing back, retrieving your previous self, isn't so simple. Sometimes that change is a permanent one.

I'm surprised I've lasted this long.

***

I found it incredibly difficult to listen to the recording of the 911 call when they played it at the trial. I have thought about that seven-minute recording an awful lot over the years. The thin, shaken sound of my voice begging the operator for help. The sporadic, gasping gaps of silence, of static, before the ambulance arrived, and the different sounds embedded in those gaps. I still think about it, wonder what I could have done differently. Whether maybe I could have done or said something that might have altered what followed.

Or what came before.

I was a good child, a good student; a good son and a good brother. And then suddenly I was not.

***

Even after the trial and the sentencing, I clung to hope for a long time. Hope that the initial appeals would see me exonerated. It was the only thing that kept me going through that first year or so, when each day was a living hell, when everyone I encountered seemed to want to hurt and abuse and humiliate me.

I'd been in fights before, schoolyard stuff, just childish scraps... But those other kids were like feral dogs, and I was easy prey. There is a

79

reason they call it Gladiator School.

But when I was finally transferred to a proper prison, I found that I received a modicum of respect. Or perhaps not that, but something else that at the time, initially, I couldn't quite understand. Not that a kid like me was given an easy ride, thrust into the world of professional felons – not at all – but I soon realised that the worse your crime was, the more people would leave you alone.

And so I learned to stop telling people that I was innocent. That I didn't kill my brother. My only relief from this was when my parents visited, not that the visits themselves were all that relieving.. In those first years I used to cry as soon as I saw them. I would tell them I didn't do it, that I needed to get out of there, and they would try to reassure me.

I would try not to, but I would bawl, and sometimes so would they. My dad would, at least.

My mother I think has been in some sort of long-lasting, permanent shock since the day her youngest son died and her eldest was locked up. Her resting face is now the definition of heartbreak itself.

Not that she has ever been cold or unloving, but there is a definite distance there. And because my father's love for me, and for Jacob, was always – and remains – so inordinately strong, her love seems in some way dimmed in comparison. When she lost Jacob, I think that much of the love in her was lost too.

My dad though, still, tells me he is going to get me out, that he loves me and believes me and will get me out. Every week he says it. But it's been a long time since I've cried in front of them, or begged them to find a way to set me free.

I've accepted that this is it, that I will most likely die in here, and that once I am gone I will very quickly be forgotten. Which is both terrifying and a comfort at the same time.

***

The others, when they don't call me by my name, sometimes call me Professor. Another example of prisoners' need to categorise themselves and each other, to delineate in a world where each man is a number.

Reading is the sole pleasure available to me. I even finished my schooling in here, even got a degree. I am probably the most educated man in my admittedly small population. Not that I will ever be able to put it to real use. But I can lose myself, however briefly, in the act of learning, of trying to understand new things.

I am fascinated by the universe, even though my mind can't fully grasp its intricacies. (This obsession with the unseen ingredients of existence comes from my mother, I think, who has always had a head full of numbers and calculations, a mind running on zeros and ones.)

I have learned, for example, that the moon is constantly spinning farther and farther away from the earth, all the time, as if it's trying to escape. Only by 2.5 inches a year, but still – that type of very slow and precise stretching of universal elements resonates, somehow.

I often try to remember what I was like – what my *mind* was like; how it worked, how I felt – when I was fifteen. When the moon was a full metre closer to us all. And with each year I seem to have gradually morphed into something different, almost imperceptibly, so that by now, after sixteen of these 365-day cycles, I can barely recall the man – the boy – I was to begin with.

There a lot of things like that. Things which, after so many years, you think you've gotten used to. But then it hits you, the reality of your life.

There's only so much you can do to distract yourself, and those long strings of minutes and hours and inches seem to elapse in a kind of extreme slow-motion, and reading a book, or listening to the radio, or writing letters or anything else, can only fill so many of them. And then all you have left is the dark insides of your mind, all you can do is *think*. And in a place like this, thinking is the problem.

Obsessing over your past and your present, and worst of all your future: the things that you've done, or haven't; the things that you've missed, and the length of a life left spread out ahead of you, stuck in a steel box, cut off from anything even slightly resembling normal human existence.

The term 'institutionalised' doesn't quite seem adequate. In here you are not really a person anymore. You are reduced to a number. Discarded. Just one more broken shell among a mound of shattered shingle.

***

I laugh more than I used to, though. I don't know why that is. There's nothing funny about this place, about the life that can happen you.

I mentioned that feeling of slowly-encroaching insanity from being incarcerated for so long. Reality can be so bleak, so oppressive, that the mind twists and squirms to escape it, turning you by small degrees half-mad – and probably, in the end, fully.

There are ways to escape it, of course.

All of it.

Men here do it all the time.

Bedsheets, mostly.

Someone famous once said that the only thing that kept them living was the knowledge they could end it all at any time of their choosing. I think about that often.

I would escape this unending existence. Its insistent routine, its desperate ambience, its hopeless and mind-bending infinitude. But I think of my father, who is certain of my innocence and fully believes he will live to see me released. And of my mother.

Though I catch her looking at me very strangely sometimes. It's hard to find the words for it, difficult to describe the almost telepathic quality of her gaze – and that silent stare is one that pierces, and could mean a thousand different things but really only means one. I don't think my Dad notices, but it's not just in my head. I am certain of that.

I try to imagine how she might react were she to get the call one night, from the warden. It fills my thinking, the darkest of daydreams,

She would cry, I'm sure.

But everybody cries.

In any case, I couldn't take another son from them, not their last remaining.

I am not some kind of animal.

Colleen MacMahon
England

Shortlist
Short Story

An Awfully Big Adventure

When I was seven my sister flew away with Peter Pan. I missed her very much, but I was happy knowing she would be living with the Lost Boys in their house under the ground – mending their socks, cooking their meals and telling them stories. I'd never actually seen her sew anything, or do more than make a cup of tea, but I knew she was good at reading and making up stories and I guessed she could learn the other stuff, even without mum's help. And I was certain she'd be good at fighting pirates.

She was fifteen when she left. There was a big gap in our ages (because mum had trouble getting pregnant again after Chloe), but it was nice because that made her a proper big sister and, when mum was sick after I was born, Clo looked after me a lot. I loved her more than anything in the world which is why, although I was a bit jealous that it was *her* Peter chose instead of me, I was happy for her too. Also, she knew about Peter before I did so it was only fair really. That she should go first, I mean.

I'm ten now and she hasn't come back yet, but I'm sure she will soon; I lie in bed, facing my big picture window with the curtains drawn back, and I wait for her.

This used to be a bunk bed, with me on the bottom and Clo on the top, but mum and dad took the top bed away about a year after she left. I didn't want them to because she'll need it back, but then I think it will be lovely – that first night of her return – for her to snuggle in with me and tell me all about Neverland and her adventures. There might be a problem, though, if Peter wants to swap us straight away and take me off that same night. I won't be able to put him off, you see, because Clo says he's notoriously unreliable and, if I send him away and ask him to come back the next night instead, he almost certainly won't.

On my bedside table I have the book with it all in. It is the proper, full length version with original illustrations. Mum says you should always read what the author originally wrote, not something somebody else has made shorter just to make it easier. If someone had cut bits out of Peter Pan it would be like visiting just part of the island instead of all of it. I don't know if J.M. Barrie ever went to Neverland or actually met Peter himself, I get the feeling he didn't because there's something about the way he writes that's sad almost. Clo said he was wistful, which I think is rather like wishful, so maybe, like us, he'd heard all about it from someone else and really, really wanted to go there but couldn't because he was too old.

Anyway, Clo always wanted to see it for herself and, of course, so did I when she started reading the book out loud to me when I was little.

Sometimes we'd dress up as Tiger Lily or Tinker Bell or Captain Hook. Once, Chloe went to a fancy dress party as a lady pirate, she looked really pretty but dad shouted at her and told her she looked like a slut and to cover herself up. She did, but she told me later that she'd changed clothes in a park on her way to the party. I think that was the night she met her new boyfriend and dad was cross about him too.

Anyway, it wasn't long after that night that Clo flew away with Peter. It was a Saturday and I remember that the whole day had a funny feeling about it. Nobody wanted to talk at breakfast and I didn't understand why. I know Clo was tired because she'd been crying the night before and didn't want to tell me what was wrong. She kept telling me to go to sleep but I was worried about her; I climbed up onto her bed and cuddled her and stroked her hair till she stopped crying. Shall I tell you a story, I asked. No, she said, I'm tired of stories. They're just like lies really, she told me, just stuff to make us feel better for a while but it doesn't last.

But I carried on talking anyway, while she stared out of the window and kind of shuddered every now and then.

I talked about Peter of course. How he was out there somewhere looking for our house, peeping through windows until he found the right one. And then one night he'd land on our window ledge, press up against the glass and look right in at us. And we'd run to open the sash and let him in. I couldn't wait for it to happen – for him to sprinkle us with the fairy dust and teach us how to fly. I had wished so hard for that moment for so long that I knew exactly how it would happen. We had no big dog like Nana to bark and wake our parents up, so we'd have all the time in the world to bump around the bedroom till we got it right. Then I would grab my teddy bear, just like Michael did in the book, and we would stand on the ledge and leap into the air. It would be the most wonderful feeling ever.

Then Chloe made me cry. He's not real, she said. Who, I asked. Peter Pan, stupid – he's just a character some pathetic old bloke made up to seduce children and keep them dreaming.

I cried, not because I believed her – I *knew* Peter Pan was real and that she was lying, but because she had said it. Why would she want to say something so horrible and untrue. I even wondered, for a moment, if she said it to put me off watching and waiting for him so that she would have a better chance. But then she said sorry, held me really tight and kissed the top of my head. I fell asleep in her arms and when I woke on the Saturday morning she was lying in exactly the same position – eyes wet and wide open and staring out into space.

That night I wanted to sleep in her bed again but she wouldn't let me. She tucked me into the bottom bunk and read to me for a while before going downstairs. I could hear her voice arguing against mum and dad's and then the television went on very loudly – I've learned that it's something grown ups do to pretend all the shouting has been the T.V. all the time. I tried to stay awake for Clo but I couldn't. A long time later, I heard her come into the room and close the curtains; I wanted to say – Don't! We won't see him if he comes! But I was too sleepy. I felt her kiss my cheek and whisper goodnight and then it sounded like she was quietly opening and closing cupboards and drawers for a while before suddenly it was morning.

I don't know how she saw him come to the window because when I woke up the curtains were still drawn across, but anyway she had gone.

I tried to explain to my parents what had happened, but they just kept hugging me and crying and telling me everything would be alright. Of course, I knew it would be; but they were really worried and unhappy. They called the police, rang all Clo's friends and dad went out to look for her. For days the phone kept ringing, people came to the door and we were even on television with mum and dad begging Chloe to come home. I felt very sad for them but, in the end, I gave up trying to tell them about Peter because they just wouldn't listen.

I knew she'd be okay, but I didn't know how long it would be before she came back. I suppose I thought she'd be like Wendy and eventually she would miss us all so much she would ask Peter to bring her home. Every night I read some of the book, it made me feel closer to her – imagining her swimming with the mermaids or sewing Peter's shadow back on or arguing, as I was sure she would, with Tinker Bell.

I would lie awake listening to the clock ticking and wondering if she'd seen the Crocodile yet. I'd always liked the Crocodile, I think he was my favourite after the boy himself.

The bit Chloe always said she liked best was the part I hated, when Peter gets taken to Marooners' Rock and is left to drown. It gets very dark and scary before he gets saved but Chlo loved it when he said, "To die will be an awfully big adventure." She said she felt the same and that upset me.

Anyway, it's three years since she left. I have new curtains now but I always keep them drawn open, even on the moonlit nights which are so bright I can't get to sleep. In fact, those are the nights when I think it's most likely that she'll come home because it'll be easier for her to find her way back. Mum and Dad talk about her a lot, blaming themselves and wondering if it was their fault she ran away. They still put up posters, make appeals on facebook and use the computer to guess how she would look now, at eighteen.

But of course, I know she doesn't look any different. And I know that, even if she never comes home, at least she will never grow old.

Eileen Merriman
New Zealand

Shortlist
Short Story

Redemption

(I)

"J'aime ta nouvelle coupe."

Dominique was sitting in the University Union Bar with Mandy and Vanessa when he walked up to her, just like that. With his mane of curly blonde hair and golden eyes, he was like a lion.

Dominique arched an eyebrow at him.

"I like the way you *don't* cut your hair." But she was pleased, because she wasn't sure if she liked her new very-short haircut, and also because he'd complimented her in her native tongue.

J'aime ta nouvelle coupe: I like your new haircut.

"It's the source of my super-powers," he said, and extended his hand. "Henry Mortimer. You're doing English lit, right?" He bought her a cider, and told her he'd learnt French for four years at high school. He told her he was a law student. He told her he had an IQ of 190.

Later, they wove between the oaks in the Domain, kicking up flurries of autumn leaves. Her friends were ahead of them, out of sight, their laughter barely audible.

Henry took her by the hand and they spun in circles, faster and faster, until they fell over. He kissed her, slowly, and whispered,

"Dominique, *ma petite poupée.*"

My little doll.

They tangled together, hands over clothes, hands under clothes, flushed skin contacting flushed skin. As he entered her, she tilted her head back to let him kiss the base of her throat. Instead, he reached for her scarf and wrapped it, ever so gently, around her neck.

"Ma petite poupée," he murmured. "I'm going to show you something that will blow your mind."

(II)

91

The day Doctor Lucy Reynolds diagnoses a murderer with a potentially curable cancer, he says, "I think we're going to be seeing a lot of each other."

They are sitting in a clinic room in Oncology Outpatients. His guard (courtesy of the forensic unit, medium-sized and blank-faced) doesn't move. Henry Mortimer (overweight and pale-faced) smiles at her. Lucy averts her gaze.

"You'll be having chemotherapy every three weeks, six cycles in total," she says. "We'll repeat your scan after four cycles, to make sure it's working."

"What if I don't want treatment?"

Lucy looks up. Henry's coppery eyes lock on hers.

"Well," she says, her heart thumping, "then you'll die, within the next few months."

"Well," he echoes, his gaze not straying from hers, "then I choose death."

She glances at the minder, but he is still blank. Thirty- nine years old, and a murderer, she should be happy he has chosen death. But in the doctor in her won't let it go.

"This is curable. You could lead a normal life."

Henry's lips part, and for the first time she notices his even, white teeth; the symmetry of his facial features. If he loses twenty kilograms, he might even be attractive.

"A normal life." His tone is mocking.

She flushes. "A long life."

Henry spreads his hands. She looks away. This conversation is nonsensical. He has already spent the last fifteen years in a forensic facility, and will never be released. Why should he care about living a long time?

Lucy takes a deep breath.

"I just need to make sure you understand the implications of your decision."

"Doctor Lucy," he says, his voice even. "Can I call you Doctor Lucy?"

She nods.

"How will I die?"

Putting her pen down, she says, "The cancer will continue to grow. It will eventually block off the outflow from your kidneys, blood vessels and other structures. There will be pain."

"Can you treat my pain?"

"There are – yes, we can treat your pain. We can keep seeing you, and treat you in a palliative fashion. That means with treatments that won't prolong your life."

"That's what I want," he says. "That's what I deserve."

***

Lucy cuts through the Domain on her way home from work, the papery leaves coating her boots. She's looked him up on the Internet of course. The younger, thinner Henry was charming, good looking, had come from a wealthy background. The creeping psychosis went unnoticed amongst his university peers and tutors, until it was too late. When questioned, Mortimer had said the sex had been consensual, the strangulation an erotic act gone fatally wrong.

A psychotic illness of the grandiose and paranoid type.

She shivers, and buttons her coat up to her neck. Henry Mortimer is right. He deserves to die.

***

Once a fortnight. That's how often she agrees to see him, to track the progress of the tumour in his abdomen, the tumour that has already caused him to lose ten kilograms in weight.

"Are you in pain?" Palpating his stomach, Lucy detects a vague fullness she hadn't noticed two weeks ago. Henry, arms by his sides, blinks up at her.

"It aches a bit. They give me paracetamol, and it goes away."

She steps back, indicating he can get dressed.

"If that's not enough, you could try some codeine" Escaping to the sanctity of her chair, she is aware of how small the clinic room is.

Henry sits up, buttoning his shirt.

"Is that addictive? I don't want anything that's addictive."

"If it's for pain, you won't get addicted." Strange how often she has to reassure her patients of that fact. Her eyes stray toward Karl, the minder. His face is impassive, as blank as ever. He is smaller than Henry. What use will he be, if Henry attacks her?

"I don't smoke," Henry says, tucking his shirt into his jeans. "Or drink."

"You're unlikely to get addicted," she reiterates, about to add that it doesn't matter, considering he'll be dead within three months. But

93

something about Henry's pose is getting to her. Maybe the way his hands are twisting in his lap, or the unsquaring of his shoulders.

"Do you have any family?" she asks.

Henry's eyes cloud over.

"My father's dead. My mother –" He shakes his head. "I don't have any family. Not anymore."

She nods in reply, because there's no response that seems appropriate. Then she writes a progress note in his file, for his psychiatrist, and shows Henry and the mindless minder out of the room.

It strikes her that Henry will die alone.

She's not sure why that should bother her. But it does.

***

Every two weeks, Lucy dutifully records Henry's symptoms (loss of appetite, abdominal discomfort, night sweats) and signs (weight loss, the enlarging mass in his abdomen). The transition from endomorph to ectomorph is slow but steady. His facial features become more defined, and with the shedding of weight he appears to shed years too.

"How long do you think it will take?" Henry asks one frigid Friday afternoon. In dark blue jeans and a white button-down shirt, he almost looks like the lawyer he could have been.

Lucy thinks she was right, about the twenty kilograms. If she didn't know about his past, she might have thought him attractive. If she didn't know he was dying. If he wasn't her –

She clears her throat. "A few weeks, two months at the most. Have you got enough pain relief?"

"I think so." Henry's always hazy about his pain. She's never really sure how much he holds back from her. "I was thinking of making a list of things I want to do before I die."

"That sounds like a good thing to do." She wonders what's on his list. She wonders how many wishes a criminally insane person in a forensic unit could possibly fulfil before they die. Very few, she imagines.

But is he really insane, anymore?

Henry laughs. "Obviously there won't be any trips to Disneyland on my list."

"Obviously," she says, the heat rising to her cheeks. Sometimes she feels like he can see every thought inside her head. "Well, I'd be interested in seeing your list, if you don't mind showing it to me."

"Oh no," he says, his eyes hazy again. "No, I don't mind at all."

94

She reminds him of Dominique, *ma petite poupée.* Lucy, however, is blonde, older, more intelligent. Not as intelligent as he, though. Not many are. He retains every morsel of information he can glean from her, turning them over in his head like pearls.

Lucy likes cycling, and fine art.

Lucy has a cat.

Lucy is single.

The day he arrives without Karl, he senses that she is a little uneasy, although her discomfort is not as obvious as it was the first day they met.

"He went to the toilet," he tells her. "He's not well. Perhaps he needs a doctor." He smiles at her, and she smiles back.

"Not a doctor like me, I hope," she says, her shoulders losing some of their tension.

"I hope so too."

No, Karl doesn't need an oncologist. A forensic pathologist, maybe.

Karl had scarcely made a noise, when Henry had choked him in the car park. Ten seconds to render him unconscious, five minutes to ensure he wouldn't be moving anytime soon.

"Do you want me to wait for him?" Henry asks, hovering in the doorway. "I can sit in the waiting room."

Lucy shakes her head. "No, it's OK. Just leave the door open."

"Thank you." He takes the chair next to her desk, as always. Lucy's hair is tied up, exposing the delicate line of her neck. Her blue shirt brings out the cornflower tones in her eyes. The transition from mutual respect to attraction has been slow but steady. He feels it now, the thrum of the force between them.

Lucy opens his file. "How are you?"

"I'm not so bad," he lies. The gnawing in his gut is constant, distracting. His bowels haven't moved for four days. And yet, excitement flickers in his weary brain.

"Did you make your list?"

He digs into his pocket, and pulls out his notebook.

"I did. Do you want to hear it?"

"Sure," she says, and after he has read out the third wish, *I'd like to tell my mother I'm sorry,* she moves to push the door to. Not closed, but so no one can peer through the crack and see that he is crying.

"You're a bit of a poet, aren't you?" Lucy says, once he has read her the wish list, the entire list bar one.

"A poet? Maybe. I used to write them, before." He catches her eye. She doesn't look away. "I think I need a prayer before dying," he says. "Do you know any?"

"A prayer before dying?" Her voice softens. "How about *Now I Lay Me Down to Sleep*?"

"That's perfect," he says, noting how his smile is mirrored in hers. The thrumming in his ears is louder now. Surely she can hear it too.

"Now I lay me down to sleep," she begins. He closes his eyes, listening. The locus of control has shifted from doctor to patient, but she doesn't know, not yet.

"I pray the Lord my soul to keep." Her voice wavers. *"If I should die before I wake, I pray the Lord my soul to take."*

Henry sighs, and looks down at his hands.

"Do you think I'll go to hell?" His heart beats faster, louder, stronger.

"I think anyone can redeem themselves," she says softly.

"Yes," he says, looking into her shimmering eyes, deep like ocean. "Yes, I think you're right."

He wants to tell her, then, why he was never attracted to alcohol or drugs or cigarettes. He wants to tell her about a rush that is more powerful than cocaine, and how a single mistake can irrevocably change the course of one's life. But he thinks it might scare her, so he decides to show her instead.

Lucy barely has time to part her lips before he has moved behind her, and clapped his hand over her mouth.

"Ma petite poupée," Henry murmurs, pulling her scarf off the back of the chair. "I'm going to show you something that'll blow your mind."

***

It's all in the timing.

Katy Wimhurst
England

Shortlist
Short Story

All for Ella

Crossing the square, I go past clowns on stilts, fire breathers, stalls selling Prozac candy floss, and riot police. EnCorp bills the Lottery as a public festival. Festival? What crap!

Outside EnCorp Guildhall the crowd thickens and I elbow my way up the steps. Inside the lobby are all the Entrance Kiosks, each the size of a small shed and with a thick metal door. Pictures of hearty workers decorate their sides, queues of thin, harrowed people stand in front. My palms are sweating as I join the shortest queue.

The newspaper of the man in front has the headline: "Extremists Demand Fair Pay and Free PsychoBliss Drops." Who believes this claptrap? I text Ella: "At Guildhall. Waiting to go in."

She replies: "Hey Ali. Sod EnCorp! Btw we're out of caffeinated ice-cream."

I drum irritably on my left thigh with my fingers, a habit Ella dislikes.

She isn't allowed to do the Lottery this year – she's got Disaffection Disorder and Infirmity of Purpose. The shrink report says they're curable, she should be better in a year. As if. It's not her fault, but I have to provide for us both. She didn't even wish me luck when I went to the bedroom to say goodbye earlier. Her face reddened and she pushed something under the duvet – maybe that locked wooden box she doesn't think I know about, which she hides under the bed. What's she keeping from me?

I wait in the queue, scanning the anxious faces behind me. They don't seem real, but nothing about the Lottery does: it's like watching a crap Channel 55 sci-fi film directed by a sociopath.

After twenty minutes my turn comes. As I walk in the Entrance Kiosk, the metal door slides closed behind me with an icy clink. There's a smell of stale sweat and broken dreams.

At the desk, the female EnCorp official demands my ID card and scans it into the computer. "Anything to declare, Miss Fisher?"

From the inner pocket of my coat, I take out a gold ring, my late Mum's wedding band, which Dad wanted me to have. I didn't tell Ella I was bringing it; she would have stopped me. But what else was there? I feel a stab of sadness as the official pockets it.

"Tell me now, please," I say.

She leans towards me conspiratorially. "Choose pink. Higher numbers better," she says.

I examine her face: I can't tell if she is lying. Bribing EnCorp officials always carries a risk.

She returns my ID card. "Go through. You're permitted fifteen minutes only by the pool or you lose your choice."

Choice? What bullshit!

In the vast hall, a banner hanging from the ceiling reads: "EnCorp Wishes You a Good Lottery: Seize the Moment!"

I shake my head. Fancy kidding myself that I'm in control! Dad, who grew up in the time before EnCorp, still can't get his head round the Lottery. Mind you, from what I've read, having a choice of work back then wasn't all it was cracked up to be, at least not for the plebs.

I walk across the hall. EnCorp changes the way the Lottery is done each year, supposedly making it 'fun'. A huge paddling-pool full of water stands at the hall's centre. Floating on the surface are thousands of rubber ducks – red, blue, green, yellow, pink, purple and white ones. I take a butterfly net from a basket and head to the poolside with a sigh. People snatch at the rubber ducks with their nets. Stocky security guards mill around.

A gaunt man with bloodshot eyes hurls his net into the pool. "This is ridiculous," he shouts. He's bundled away by security guards to a Public Penance Trampoline. A dozen trampolines are in the hall, all in use.

Last year Ella had to bounce for telling a security guard where to shove the Lottery. Ella can't keep her mouth shut: that's the difference between us.

One woman bouncing wears a blue cassock. As she jumps up and down, it billows and shrinks like a swimming jellyfish. She speaks through a loud-hailer: "We're not worthy." Bounce. "Need to better ourselves." Bounce. "Work hard." Bounce. "Work sets us free."

100

Bounce.

She *must* be PR for EnCorp.

To my right, two women have hold of the same purple rubber duck. "Give it me," hisses one. "Mine, you bitch," spits the other. They are dragged away by security guards. Nothing that happens in this stupid Lottery surprises me.

I net four pink rubber ducks. A bloke beside me stares at the pool, scratching his long beard. "Symbolic, innit," he says. "Life's a sodding lottery."

"But the game's rigged," I say.

I check which rubber duck is labelled with the highest number, hold on to that, and chuck the others back. After dumping the butterfly net in a basket, I queue at an Exit Kiosk. The grey-haired woman in front of me clenches her red rubber duck tightly to her chest. I move my pink one fretfully from one hand to the other; the armpits of my tee-shirt are clogged with sweat.

In the Exit Kiosk, an EnCorp official takes the rubber duck, taps its number into his computer, and prints a small Job Allocation Card. "What job?" I ask.

"Seen worse." He hands it to me.

Without reading the card, I hurry outside. Endgame Square is full: a few people are celebrating, many sit slumped, some try to swap jobs, flashing cards at each other. A public tannoy system plays *We're All Monday's Heroes*. I hate that song.

I take a deep breath and read my Job Card: five ten-hour night-shifts a week as a Senior Warehouse Supervisor at the EnCorp Knitting Emporium. I let out a sigh. Nights aren't great – travel can be dangerous – but this is regular work, not zero-hours. The money will cover rent, food, electricity and the occasional emergency or treat. Working nights I'll get time to read too. Handing over Mum's ring was worth it. I allow myself a brief smile.

Without Ella I'd manage okay on this money, even be able to visit Dad up north or have luxuries occasionally – a dark chocolate Munchbomb, a bottle of Alcoheaven. Why am I thinking this? Ella has no one else.

How will she handle me being gone most nights? She woke shouting from a nightmare at 3am again. "S'okay," I said, stroking her hair. "Just a dream."

I better get going and tell her about the job.

A teenager approaches. "Wanna swap? Money's good," she says. Beneath her pensive eyes, her purple lipstick is smudged.

"What've you got?"

"City prostitute."

"Behind EnCorp Head Office?"

She nods, grimacing.

Poor kid. The elite there are sadists. "What's the pay?" I ask.

"Two thou" a month." She shows me her card.

Could I do it? On that money Ella and I would be able to save up a bit, maybe even get out of the city.

Ella would hate me doing it. "You can't have sex with those bastards," she'd say. "They screw us enough as it is." She's right of course, and there'd be the medical bills for stitches and antibiotics.

"Sorry, no," I say. "Is this your first lottery?"

"Ner, I'm seventeen." Her chin juts up. "Gotta find a swap."

"You will. Keep asking around."

As I walk away, I look round Endgame Square. The atmosphere is tense: stalls are doing a bustling trade in Mogadon smoothies and Prozac candy floss; cards are torn up, fights break out, security guards and riot police muscle in. The ten Penance Trampolines are in use; spectators hurl things at the bouncers – insults, apple cores, rubber ducks.

There'll be a riot soon. Always is. For years I hung around because the riot was cathartic. Now I have Ella to think of.

I join the stream of people leaving the square, pausing on Adcart Bridge to look at the river. Fake plastic trout, suspended from tiny floats, glow in pinky silver just beneath the surface. It's weirdly pretty.

A muscular bloke in a tight white tee-shirt, probably an undercover policeman, stops and gives me the eye. "Done the Lottery, darlin'?" he asks.

My shoulders tense, I offer a curt nod.

"Fancy a bit of fun?" His fat-slug eyebrows rise up.

As I turn away, he grabs my wrist. "I know a cheap PleasureDome," he says.

"Let go. Please."

His grip tightens. My wrist hurts. "Get off me," I insist.

Passers-by look the other way. He tugs me closer and whispers,

"C'mon, blondie. You know you want it."

"Let go or I'll fucking well scream."

As he releases me, he spits in my face. "Stupid tart. Too skinny anyway."

I flinch, and then hurry away, wiping off the disgusting spit with my sleeve. I glance back to check he's not following.

My pulse has returned to normal when I enter the cheap frozen food warehouse on Mercy Street. I hope they still sell ice-cream: last week the bakery next-door was selling second-hand laptops, tinned fruit, and recycled teddy bears. I'm relieved to find caffeinated ice-cream, Ella's favourite. I try to make her eat healthily, but she turns her pretty nose up. "Who cares what I eat?" she says.

"You're on medication. You need something healthy."

"Bugger that."

"You'll get fat."

"I'm fat already. You like fat women."

True, I do.

As I come out on Mercy Street, several people pelt past and a few seconds later a riot policeman hurtles by. "Stop or I'll shoot!" He fires a shot without waiting. A woman squeals and falls, clutching her leg.

A siren goes off somewhere, my pulse races. Time I got away.

People start to panic and run. I walk hurriedly and, just past Cheapskates, hang a right into Eden's Passage. Worried shop-keepers are pulling down metal grates on shop-fronts. I nip down the narrow alley beside Budget Drugs. You have to know the area well to know this cut-through. Ella worked in that shop one year, calls it Budget Drudge. Two women are ahead, one glances back. I wave to show I'm friendly; she nods. We all hurry down to the end, coming out in Darkhorse Lane, where there's hardly anyone. I should be okay from here.

Forty minutes brisk walk brings me home to Worn Road, which has more potholes than tarmac. Half-way down the road I stop abruptly. In the decaying oak are two parrots with kingfisher-blue and bright-yellow feathers. How beautiful! I've seen parrots here before, but not like this and not for ages. I smile and shake my head before setting off again.

The stairwell in our block stinks of mould and pee. Ella and I want to leave here, but it's impossible. You need about a couple of thousand quid to bribe officials for a Flat Move Visa.

As I open the front door, I say, "Hey."

No answer.

I check the flat. No Ella. She rarely goes out alone. Maybe she's popped down to the shop?

I make myself a cup of tea and wait. I look at the wall-clock with its broken minute hand, then at my Job Card, imagining Ella's face when she sees it.

An hour passes. I make another cup of tea. Pace the room. Try to read my book, but can't concentrate. Where is she?

In the bedroom, I look for Ella's locked little box, under the blankets in the case beneath the bed. I take it out: pine with a spiral engraved clumsily on the top, and unlocked for once. I hesitate, then flip the lid open. Nothing. Has she taken whatever was in it? Is she okay? I rush to the bathroom cabinet, check her pills. Still there. My relief is brief. I pace the flat once more.

An hour later, the front door opens. Ella enters, dark rings underscore her eyes. "Hey," she says.

"Where the hell have you been?"

"Keep your hair on, woman."

"I thought you'd be waiting to find out about my job." I say this curtly.

She frowns. "Is the job… shit?"

"Actually, the money's okay. Look!" I hand her my card.

She holds it, staring, and then glances up. "Nights."

"Sorry. I know they're your bad times."

"I'm more worried about *you* travelling. But this money *is* okay." There's a flicker of a smile on her face.

I hold up my shopping bag. "I got caffeinated ice-cream."

"My favourite! I've got something to show you, too." From her pocket she pulls out a Job Card.

Surprised, I take it: reception work at Pluto's Tombstone Warehouse. Not bad money either. "How the hell did you get this?"

"I did the Lottery." She shows me a false ID: her photo but in the name of Emma Fischer.

"Where on earth…?"

"There *are* ways to game the system." She straightens her spine and pats herself playfully on the chest, then lets out a sigh. "Well, I pawned Gran's gold pearl necklace and earrings to get it. Been hiding it in a box under the bed. I wanted to surprise you."

"But you're banned from working. The shrink's report—"

"The shrink's report can piss off. That egotistical dimwit couldn't handle the fact I'm mouth. And smart."

Ella can be all bravado, but underneath she's vulnerable. I gaze at her face, feisty and fragile.

"I know I struggle with my mood, Ali, but who doesn't? Being cooped up here all day is driving me gaga."

"What if EnCorp rumble you?"

"As if. They may be bastards, but they're incompetent bastards."

She may have a point, but I'm still uneasy.

"I'll take the risk," she says. "With both our pay checks, we'll be able to save up, maybe get out of the city next year. Find ourselves a little flat by the sea up north, near your Dad. Imagine! You've always wanted to live by the sea." Her long, unkempt, black hair is haloed by the soft afternoon light from the window, a glint surfaces in her large, brown eyes, her lips curl into a wonky smile.

It's a smile that swells my heart, makes life so real and tender. "Come here, Emma Fischer," I say.

Her lips part as she steps towards me.

Poetry Report

Being on the judging panel for MOLP is something I really look forward to; it's such a privilege to read these new pieces of work which always evoke a whole rainbow of emotions and a great deal of respect for the authors and their craft.

Poetry is a demanding form; it requires absolute precision and in that precision lies a quiet beauty. There is very little, if any, of the leeway that prose can afford; every word has to count and to carry its weight. It's as if you must distil that moment, those circumstances, that set of emotions into one perfect, shimmering drop. And that's just the start, for of course there are many, many different poetic forms and then there's rhythm to think about, flow and cadence, possibly rhyme, maybe assonance... Phew!

Literary alchemy on a grand scale.

And here again, the MOLP entrants are courageous and intrepid alchemists; they have tackled a wide variety of subjects in a multitude of forms (please don't ask me to name them all – I'll fail miserably!) and given the judging panel a really tough job. We'd like to thank all of you for your entries; even if you didn't make it onto the shortlist, there wouldn't be a competition without you and the Word Forest would be so very much smaller.

The five poems that made it onto the shortlist are, in alphabetical author name order, Daddy Longlegs by John Harley, Transfiguration by Neil Harrison, The Opera Glasses by Michele Mills, Counting Backwards by Lisa Reily and For My Father by Nina Watson.

Daddy Longlegs by John Harley is an exquisitely observed piece which shines a sympathetic light upon its unusual subject and serves up some wonderful description. It also calls up some intriguing parallels between

106

human and insect which are delightfully thought provoking.

Stunning celestial metaphors are peppered through Transfiguration, a captivating picture of a murmuration of starlings. Neil catches them in an elegant and clean style and his light touch carries you effortlessly up on the wings of the creatures themselves.

It can be tricky to write about nostalgia and loss without being over sentimental but Michele pulls it off brilliantly in The Opera Glasses. Direct language in a series of short lines creates pace through a deeply poignant moment. This is a tender and touching stanza.

There is a delicious humour at the beginning of Lisa's Counting Backwards; anyone who has had surgery will recognise the thoughts and feelings of the central character. The emotion deepens and darkens as the poem draws to its conclusion, leaving the reader with a lump in the throat.

For my Father is insightful and deeply moving. Nina's calm, even tone beautifully counterpoints the desperation that her powerful imagery conjures. Potent observation combined with subtlety and reserve create emotional dynamite in this compassionate poem.

The top five prize winners of MOLP 4 are Mistook by Jonathan Greenhause and Definition of a Tree by Susan Rogerson, who both received £50 and a highly commended accreditation. In third place, winning £100 was The Old Man's Grave by Malcolm Deakin. Cherries by Judy Drazin took the second prize of £300 while the first prize of £1,000 went to Orca by Dee Barron.

Jagged lines and a marvellous use of assonance create a palpable sense of panic in Mistook. Jonathan's sensuous and inventive language paints vivid and unusual images which linger long in the mind and will leave you wanting to dash up the beach to aid of this wonderful creature.

Using all fifty permitted lines, Susan took on a subject that is popular amongst MOLP entrants and nailed it with Definition of a Tree. With lush and evocative imagery, she brews a wonderful concoction of reality and mythology; you will feel drawn to find a tree and sit quietly beneath it, contemplating anew these vital lungs of our planet.

Cherries is a beautiful, melancholic love poem which captures most heartrendingly the loss of a beloved and the bittersweet memories that simple, mundane objects can evoke. Judy has set down an ordinary moment and skilfully made it extraordinary, expanding what is a hard and emotionally charged task into a poignant memoir. Her deceptively simple style paints a series of vivid portraits and the last will stay with you for days.

The Old Man's Grave is a brilliantly realised mesh of poetic form. This ballad ensnared me from the start and wouldn't let go; the exuberant pace gallops along like the boulder it describes. Malcolm's clever use of rhyme never seems forced (which is no mean feat!) and his rich, pleasingly formal language in a regular rhythm (8 syllable triplets with a 7 syllable fourth line) draws the reader ever on to the thought provoking conclusion. It's not hard to imagine a Shakespearian actor delivering this on stage at the Globe. Superb.

Orca provides a shocking and abhorrent snapshot of our time. Dee's choice of point of view highlights the cruelty that humans are capable of, capturing the claustrophobia and stress that incarceration visits on the orca in a way that will make your blood run cold. Her minimalist approach creates maximum impact; short lines, some just two syllables, amplify the horror and hopelessness of the situation. An eloquent wake up call, this is poetry that can kick start real change. An exceptional piece of writing and a most worthy winner.

Having had the privilege of reading through these beautifully crafted pieces of writing, I recommend that you carve out a special piece of time to immerse yourself fully in them.

Kufurahia! Asante sana!

Izzy Robertson
Judge

Dee Barron
England

1st Prize - Poetry

Dee was born in Southampton, Hampshire but moved to sunny Swanage, Dorset, fifteen years ago where she lives with her partner. She says that they are truly blessed to be surrounded by such beautiful landscape and they venture outdoors as much as they can to appreciate it, both by land and sea.

She has always enjoyed the Arts and during student/working years, Dee studied 20th Century Art and Literature with the Open University. Some of her favourite poets include Larkin and Auden.

It might surprise people to know that for over 30 years she has worked in the insurance profession!

Orca

How many more
Will file past my liquid cell
To stare
Wide-mouthed
Like senseless fish,
Flat, fleshy faces
Pressed hard against the glass
Of my captivity,
To point
To poke
And to pry?

How many more
Will spread the lie
That my scars will 'heal',
That my limp and lifeless fin
Is merely 'sleeping in between tricks',
That my daily fill
Of drugs and dead meat
Is 'good for a growing boy'?

How many more
Will join the squealing queue
To 'dine' with me
But have no clue
That in between those tasteless treats
I am chewing bars
And grinding teeth

And shredding skin
Over and over again
Against walls
Of maddening
Concrete
Monotony?

How many more
Will applaud
Each tedious breach
And cheer when water-
Still haunted by the spirits
Of our stillborn-
Slaps hard
Across scores of smiling faces?

And how many will come
To mourn my death
When my final breath
Brings the night crane
To winch me out of sight
And away
From the spinning turnstiles
Of another day?

How many more?

Judy Drazin
England

2nd Prize
Poetry

Cherries

One morning, energised by
grief, I set to polishing your
desk, it being my
bitter pleasure, to safe
guard the shining.
Huddled as if for comfort
in a drawer, the thinning
flotsam of your life,
a favoured watch, binoculars,
a silver paper knife.

Your uncased glasses seem
defenceless at first touch
but gentled in my hand
they gain in strength.
Boldly I slip them on and
watch the memories
uncurl, grandchildren,
still in bud, picnics in fields
made generous with blackberries,
a pretty daughter, eyes
choked up with secrets
new shoes and oh

two lovers in an orchard,
where sweet cherries grow
my dear, we used to pick them
long, long ago.

Malcolm Deakin
England

3rd Prize
Poetry

The Old Man's Grave

"It matters not" the old man said,
"Where my corpse lies when I'm dead,
I want no tombstone at my head,
nor mourners at my dying.
So take yon boulder, roll it hard,
make sure it covers yard on yard,
its resting place you must regard
as where in death I'm lying."

They gave the stone a mighty push
and watched it bounce through field and bush,
that mighty bulk increased its rush,
choosing not its going.
For nothing could impede its bounce,
that solid rock, its every ounce,
all in its path it did denounce,
uncaring, never knowing.

Down the hill the boulder rolled,
the man who lined his purse with gold,
wanted not the graveyard's mould,
all starved of isolation.
The boulder rolled on down the hill,
rolling, rolling where it will,
until at last it stopped quite still,
at nature's invitation.

It rested there beside a brook,
the old man then this life forsook,
his chapter closing as a book,
where none may know its ending.
Still and quiet all around,
men pronounced it hallowed ground,
the waiting boulder made no sound,
a restful peace descending.

Buried this old man did lie,
beneath boulder, grass and sky,
where he lived, he died, for why,
ours is not the asking.
And now he lies there all alone,
his epitaph a rolling stone,
to guard him through the great unknown,
in sweet repose he's basking.

Resting at his own command,
was it not he that owed the land,
and boulder that so came to stand,
the old man's whim to flatter?
And there he lies unto this day,
proving some will have their way,
despite what other men might say
and think "why should it matter?"

119

Susan Rogerson
England

Highly Commended
Poetry

Definition of a Tree

A lucidity of cells,
exhaled on paper wings;
spun through spirit of feather and fur;
stitched with light;
plumped by soft Spring rain.

Nut of consciousness,
bounced off woodland floor –
hidden in the crisp crunch of its own shed skin;
enfolded in pliant earth –
Held.

Pencilled thought,
drawn from Winter's depths by pluvial sun;
fattened on fungal brew –
mycelial ideas, latticed beneath view –
mooring root to root;
wind's hand shaping its scrawls
across parchment sky.

Green-sleeved guardian –
soft-edged or serrated;
deep-bevelled; precision-pointed –
charging those interleaved heartbeats
that scuttle and flit along loaded limbs;
burrow beneath skin –
their stories lining this year's nest;
patterned in insect trails across warm flesh.

Summer reassurance –
a continuity of stillness –
backrest for light reading in a crook of roots.

Autumn's gypsy,
dressed in sunset rags –
revelling in the last Solstice embers –
garments flung into flames –
dancing naked – arms outstretched
to the boreal wind.

Footbridge linking worlds –
roots tunnelling through sand; clay; rock –
entwining with antlers of Cernunnos;
pointing the way to Cerydwen's Cauldron of Truth.
Twig-tips tapping stars;
tapping souls of dead and dreamers –
ambitions scratched in rough bark.

Traveller's breath –
heartbeat pulsing through constant trunk –
strength for weary head.

Map of the world;
anchor to continental drift –
Earth's conscience ringed
within pages of the universe –
counterweight to planetary shift.

Jonathan Greenhause
United States of America

Highly Commended
Poetry

Mistook

The poorly-rested whale
wails well into the night, is trapped
in a tide-pool
with spiky starfish
resembling suns. She's the size
of sorrow,
the magnitude of a supernova,
the seamstress
of a tapestry of regret. She's
a songstress
undone by stress, done in
by lament.
The poorly-rested whale
won't rest
'til the ocean refills with
the remembrance
of her membership of whales, of
the marine equivalent
of our myth of
Eden. She paints portraitures

with her bubbles, sculpts landscapes
with her fluke,
writes romans-à-clef
with her mournful eyes, swoons
to sea shanties,
revels in the motion
of the waves,

but the poorly-rested whale
is still stuck
in the muck of what
she mistook as home, what's
newly arranged as
her shimmering tomb, unless we assume

she'll escape.

John Harley England

Shortlist
Poetry

Daddy Longlegs

There is something about you that lives in my being.
Why is it that you are always floundering?
Always trying to perform magic
by flying through glass panes
from the carpeted air of houses
to the fading summer light of the outdoors.
Your body is scribbled in the black ink of the insect world,
you shed legs carelessly behind you,
a litter of limbs,
the eyelashes of giants.
Your wings are all thread and paper
scribbled hurriedly by a tired inventor,
too flimsy to lift the tangled machinery of your frame,
convincingly.
Your head is the head of a sea horse,
elegant and curved,
black dot eyes fixed on survival
as rain holds you down
and pulls you into death.
Why do I love to trap you in my cupped hands
and feel your frenzied need to escape
vibrate against my skin?
Is there something about your foundering I understand?
Perhaps in the way your life slowly dismantles you
I can find my own struggles,
my habit of falling apart,
my desire to be free
and my dream of helicoptering up into the sky.

Neil Harrison
United States of America

Shortlist
Poetry

Transfiguration

Yesterday it was hard to swallow
old tales of daylight growing dim
under flocks of migrating birds,
but today a cloud of starlings
pouring south over Beaver Creek
affords plenty of time to wonder
who first imagined them the progeny
of those far-off lights in the heavens.

Bearing a night sky in miniature
on each of their countless bodies,
they unite under a common spirit
until no individual remains,
just this winged shadow overhead
spanning the sky, a living god.

Michele Mills
England

Shortlist
Poetry

The Opera Glasses

She gave them to me,
Last Christmas Day,
Prettily wrapped, of course,
In a silver bag,
With corded handles,
White tissue-plumped,
Gold ribbon-tied
(The thought makes me cry)
And tucked inside
A black, velvet,
Draw-string pouch.
I remembered them,
Vaguely, among all
The gorgeous things
She'd collected, over years,
About which
I'd never, really, asked,
Because, they were,
Like her, beautiful,
And always there.
Didn't I wonder
Where she'd found or
When she bought them,
How much for?
Glamorous opera glasses!
Vintage, brass lenses,
Engraved, branded
La Vogue - Paris,

Encased in iridescent,
Pink, blue-veined
Mother-of-pearl;
Such style
And, I find,
Perfectly focused,
Even through
Tear-blurred eyes.
Because, I hadn't asked
So many questions,
Presuming answers
To be always here,
Denying the day
This view on life
Would disappear.
So, what else to do,
But, look ahead
And somehow through
The dearly acquired,
Edged in brass,
Mother-of-pearl
Opera glasses?

Lisa Reily
Australia

Shortlist
Poetry

Counting Backwards

Freckled white skin, my back gapes
unavoidably
from behind a crisp tablecloth, a single string
to protect me from nakedness.
The sheet beneath me is rigid with bleach;
I thought I would feel more comfortable.

I imagine myself on your operating table,
dying,
or dead already, awaiting beautification
for our family's viewing.

I thought I'd feel less anxious, thought
I'd drift into sleep, thought
my last bed would be something special,
and personal; I've said my goodbyes, just in case.

I may not wake up, I say to myself. Today,
I surrender
my wisdom teeth and, conceivably,
my memories, my last breath,
my whole life.

I am wheeled away
by a person wearing a shower cap;
they smile and I reply with a stupid grin;
I don't care where I am,
but a gentle touch of this stranger's hand

and I am comforted, by their warmth, their voice.

I am moved to your table,
then I count back with ease, and self-confidence.
I am in their hands and I count, backwards,
with ease... backwards... *four*...
three... two... then I drift...

into nothingness...

and for a moment, I realise that *death*
is so close, so close...

and then I am gone...

I wake, bleary, mouth full of blood;
my dizziness and nausea spilled, consoled
by another stranger, their tender voice;

I am here, I am here... I am back,
but you are gone, forever.
And the strangers who took you
continue their work, carefully,
as best they can, as they should.

I imagine you here, counting backwards...
four... three... two...
as you drift into nothingness,
not knowing you would never wake;
never count birthdays beyond sixteen.

And the strangers who took you
continue their work, meticulously,
as best they can, as they should.

Nina Watson
England

Shortlist
Poetry

For My Father

I love you.
But we're sitting stiffly on borrowed days.
A throne of trepidation that can crack with one CT scan.

We do not die once,
but over and over and over again in tiny fragments.
You walk through the door and call me 'my handsome'.
One day that door will stay closed,
and on that day I will shatter slightly, shards will fall and shine on the
places I had forgotten.

The masses are not just in your body.
They block out our sun, seeping slowly like sinister rivulets souring
every conversation.
Glassy eyes and lingering embraces cannot change this.

I love you.
You love me.

But you cannot hear anything other than darkness over the crowded
humming of an MRI.

About Bunaken Oasis: Our Sponsor

We conceived Bunaken Oasis with one overriding aim in mind: to create a dive resort whose every aspect meets our own exacting requirements for quality and service, both on land and on the sea. Distilling our experiences from luxury (and not-so-luxury) resorts around the world, our refusal to compromise means that every guest - diver, snorkeller, photographer - can enjoy the treasures of Bunaken from a resort which anticipates and meets just about their every need.

Bunaken Oasis redefines diving in Bunaken. Positioned very much at the luxury end of the spectrum, our aim is to provide a 5-star experience whilst keeping our ecological footprint to a minimum.

The resort offers 12 large, traditionally-built villas, including one family villa with two bedrooms, and one villa near the Long House for those who may have difficulty walking.

A major focal point of the resort is a free form infinity pool, with sun-loungers and easy access to the bar, for those who want to spend time above, rather than below, the water.

In addition to a chill-out cocktail bar and a full-service restaurant serving Indonesian and international cuisine, guest amenities also include an air conditioned library, a fully-equipped classroom in the Dive Centre with 4k flat-screen TV, especially useful for photographic groups, and a spacious camera room with more charging points than you will ever need.

The Bunaken Marine National Park is a protected, though fragile, environment, and we are committed to taking our eco-responsibilities very seriously. Using our own bore holes, or even sea-water, with water makers and ultraviolet treatment, we have ensured that all the water in the resort is fully drinkable, and we can avoid the need for one of the greatest pollutants of our time - plastic bottles. In addition, all waste water will be processed through a water-treatment plant.

Wherever possible, we will hire Indonesian staff for all positions; when this is not possible, it will be part of the job description of the foreign incumbent to develop his or her local successor.

The resort is built on a steep hillside overlooking the mangroves on Liang Beach (don't worry, there are gently meandering paths everywhere, so getting around the resort is easy!).

Your transfer boat from the mainland will moor at our private jetty, and you'll enter Bunaken Oasis through our beautiful Long House. Above the Long House is a spectacular free form infinity pool, ideal for who might choose to relax and catch some sun rather than dive.

Moving past the pool, you come to the chill-out cocktail bar, where you can enjoy a range of fine wines and spirits (and Bintang!) while you unwind beneath the stars. To the side of the bar is our restaurant, and because you'll be spending quite a lot of time here, we've really made it something special: with fantastic views over the pool, Long House and out to sea, you'll enjoy gourmet Asian and western cuisine at breakfast, lunch and dinner.

Towards the rear of the resort is our tranquil Spa; wind down after a day's diving by choosing a massage from our extensive menu of treatments, and leave yourself in the hands of one of our fully-trained therapists.

We are proud to be associated with Magic Oxygen Publishing, another company that not only cares passionately about the environment and sustainability, but shows that it makes good business sense too.

For more information visit **BunakenOasis.com**
Twitter.com/BunakenOasis Facebook.com/BunakenOasis

Judgemental Gallery:

16 judges

from

5 countries

on

4 continents

evaluated entries

from

24 countries

Sarah Acton

Sarah is a Jurassic Coast poet whose work along the Devon and Dorset coastline flows directly from her relationship with the natural coastline and living landscape.

Sarah is the Jurassic Coast World Heritage Site poet-in-residence, a three year project spanning 95 miles of Jurassic coastline and 185 million years. The residency is hosted at local museums to create a site specific body of work inspired by the museum collections, archives and surrounding natural environment.

Sarah runs poetry workshops, poetry walks and open mic nights throughout East Devon and West Dorset, under the name of Black Ven.

Chaz E Arnold

Chaz is a Devon based author, poet and illustrator. Under his social media alias, @PaigntonPoet, he has gained a loyal following of his positive, light-hearted poetry and daily illustrations.

His latest novel, The Bone Identity, is a Jason Bourne meets Lassie spy thriller and Hope V - Kayos, the fifth instalment of The Hope Saga, is currently on the drawing board.

The highlight of Chaz's poetry career, so far, was being the sole poetry contributor to the National Trust's Spirit of Place exhibition at Buckland Abbey in Devon.

Being inspired by art is the cornerstone of Chaz's poetic creativity and he continues to work with the Devon Art Pop group.

Nick Bellorini

Nick is a non-fiction publisher based in the South West.

When not forming judgments on the literary efforts of others, he writes a little himself and is currently slowly redrafting something which might one day be a novel set in Hungary between the wars (though knowing publishing to be a bit of a crapshoot he's not placing any bets).

His literary tastes are not terribly stable and so he is very often surprised and charmed. Which is one of the pleasures of being a judge for MOLP.

Monica Ciriani

Monica is a poet and artist. She was born in Libya, from Italian parents and has lived in Italy, Vietnam, Nigeria and Scotland. She went to Dublin for a 4 day holiday and ended up living there for 13 years, but now lives in England.

The diversity of her life experiences compelled her to find ways to both express and question them.

She is attracted to a wide spectrum of literature and visual art, from tattooing and abstract expressionism to T.S. Elliot, E.E. Cummings and folk music!

She believes there are no limits to art, it is all about how you learn to see it, to feel it, and then to express it through whatever medium attracts you; anything you create must have soul.

Ru Hartwell

Born in South Africa, Ru has been planting trees for the last four decades and has run the tropical reforestation project down in Boré, Kenya since 2007.

Working in partnership with 300 Giriama subsistence farmers, he has been responsible for the planting of 170,000 trees and is overjoyed to be helping make the Magic Oxygen Word Forest a reality for this community. Every single tree is a like a little victory for nature and this great project adds up to a significant positive result for one typical African primary school, its kids and our shared atmosphere.

He doesn't have time to read a great many books these days but loves The Long Walk by Slavomir Rawicz.

Sue Jueno

Sue had a desire to make a difference began back in the 80's working for Band Aid and Sport Aid.

Later an interest in the environment led to creating the online 'My Green Directory', which she ran for 11 years. This promoted eco friendly companies only, and along with paperback versions in The Guardian and event partnerships, including The Observer Ethical Awards, luckily reached a wide audience.

Having worked in wildlife conservation for the last couple of years, Sue is delighted to be part of the judging team for this amazing, one of a kind competition especially as it will be replacing essential habitat.

Wangechi Kiongo

Wangechi is a 23 year old Kenyan with an unbeatable passion for the environment.

She is an environmentalist and has a passion for mentoring children and youths on environmental conservation issues.

She is also a wildlife researcher, and a writer and blogger, who pens pieces on environmental matters.

In 2017, Wangechi was awarded the United Nations Convention to Combat Desertification (UNCCD) Youth Land for Life Social Media Activist, where she is tasked with advocating for sustainable land management systems that support achievement of SDG 15.

Toni McKee

Toni is an ex-pat living in New Zealand having left Dorchester in Dorset in April 2017. An avid reader, she is the proud mum of a Magic Oxygen author - Connor McKee.

Currently working as a supply teacher she has also worked in schools on the Isle of Man, in Ontario, Devon and Dorset before setting up home in Ashburton on the South Island in the land of the long white cloud.

An avid supporter of all things environmental, Toni tries to walk as lightly on this mother earth of ours by reducing her consumption of resources and reusing things we have that need repairing. She grows her own fruit and veggies and hopes to keep a few chickens soon.

Cyprian Ogoti

Cyprian is an environmental journalist with a Bachelor's degree in Journalism and Media Studies. He is a seasoned content developer and avid user of social media platforms who is engaged in advocacy, water and environment issues and education.

He has over 7 years professional experience in developing written content for international development agencies and the civil society and creating content for websites, office reports, newsletters, fliers and brochures and social media.

He works with communities to confront environmental challenges they face by promoting environmental rights. He has been working in Suswa and has planted over 11,500 trees since 2015.

Sandie Roach

Sandie is a waste-hating student of life, being home educated by her three sons in the beautiful city of Whanganui, on the north island of New Zealand. She is currently studying Te Reo Maori and Social Sciences. She enjoys travel, adventure and all things new.

She loves being involved in her local community and helps facilitate Whanganui's monthly 'Really Really Free Market'.

Sandie is studying for a Social Sciences degree with Open Polytechnic. Her favorite author of the moment is Rivera Sun who penned the novel 'The Dandelion Insurrection – Love and Revolution'.

Izzy Robertson

Izzy, a keen reader for longer than she cares to admit, ate books for breakfast, lunch and dinner as a child and aspired to authordom from the age of eight.

It's taken a while, and gone via a completely different career pathway, but she now has two short stories out as e-books, her novel 'Dreaming The Moon' was published in 2015 and her second novel, 'Three Words' was published on Valentine's Day 2017.

She is also an editor, having worked on several books for Magic Oxygen including all the MOLP anthologies. She prefers the magical and mystical for reading matter; particular favourite authors include Charles de Lint and Alice Hoffman.

Jed Robertson

Jed is studying music at USW in Cardiff. As well as his musical endeavours, he enjoys writing poetry and fantasy fiction.

He has a passion for concept albums as they bring together his love for progressive music and fantasy tales with the lyrics and musical setting telling the story.

The music and lyrics of these works have been used to tell stories as epic as the myths of old as well as harrowing interpretations of real events.

Jed finds the combination of arts incredibly inspiring, as each can influence and enhance the others, He says, "What would a book be without its cover art and how could we enjoy great cinema without musical scores?"

Lata Tokhi

Lata is the Founder and Chief Editor of the hugely popular women's website, DotComWomen.com. She also curates a network of Holiday websites, including Celebrating-Chirstmas.com which has been rated 5 stars by the editors at CNET's Download.com. A doting mom of 3, she chronicles her momlife on her blog FabulousMomLife.com.

She loves to read romantic poetry, Jane Austen, and truly believes that she was a Jane Austen character in her past life! Lata has been advocating women's issues for the last 16 years through her media network.

Lata is an avid Yoga practitioner and a vegetarian. She lives with her techie husband and three kids in the beautiful country of India.

Simon Wallace

Simon taught English in a comprehensive school in north-east England for seven years.

He later formed Wallace Walker, a flourishing management consultancy.

He has run management seminars across the Middle East and in Malaysia, although his focus is now developing Bunaken Oasis Dive Resort, a luxury, eco-friendly diver's holiday resort in Indonesia.

Simon is an avid reader, but has yet to find anything to supplant 'Vanity Fair' as his desert island novel.

Andy Wright

Andy is a Toronto based, internationally acclaimed photographer - a specialist of live gigs - he is originally from London.

When he's not crawling around on the floor of events and red carpets looking for that amazing shot, he is typically crawling around on the floor of a venue shooting a band, touring with the likes of Marillion, Spock's Beard, and Sound of Contact.

He is also published and there are limited edition books packed with his fantastic images all around the globe. These include '9.30 to Filmore' and 'Marillion's Heartbeat' (co-written with Populuxe drummer Mark Pardy).

He has also created some amazing book covers for Magic Oxygen.

Tracey West FRSA - Head Judge

As well as being Chief Judge, Tracey is also CEO and Fundraiser for The Word Forest Organisation, the reforestation charity born as a direct result of this international writing competition.

"The idea of MOLP blossoming into an NGO had been brewing in my head like a strong cup of Kenyan tea, for about 6 months before I put it to Simon. Within a few weeks we'd applied to the Charities Commission and I've been officially 'at the helm' for 11 months now. They have been the most incredible days of my life! I'm so proud of what the entrants have helped us achieve over the last 4 years and I can only imagine what's going to happen in the next 4; hold tight people and keep writing!"

Simon West FRSA - Technical Guru

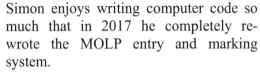

Simon enjoys writing computer code so much that in 2017 he completely re-wrote the MOLP entry and marking system.

Having adopted a vegan lifestyle at the start of 2016, his tea intake has been entirely with plant-based milk and his (vegan) chocolate habit has continued unabated.

Despite not being one of the judges, he read almost all of the entries, and was delighted to see some of his favourites in the shortlist.

Simon has been working hard with Tracey since 2016 to ensure The Word Forest Organisation is a success, and delighted in being 'the media guy' on their recent monitoring and evaluation trip to Kenya.

About Magic Oxygen

Magic Oxygen Limited is a small, green publishing house based in Lyme Regis, Dorset. It was founded in 2011 by Tracey and Simon West, who share passions for organic, seasonal, locally grown food which they enjoy turning into an adventurous array of vegan delights.

They're also advocates for simple green living, they encourage sustainable behaviours in local and global environments and they share a common love of the written word.

Magic Oxygen is also responsible for creating the greenest writing contest in the world, the only one to plant a tree for every single entry and to build classrooms in impoverished communities too. If you looked at the title page of this anthology, you will see that MOLP was the reason for Tracey & Simon starting a charity – The Word Forest Organisation. Over the next few pages Tracey will tell you all about it and some of the work it has done in Kenya.

This little literary company has published 33 titles from some outstanding authors over the last few years, including Bridport Prize winning Chris Hill and the much loved children's writer, Sue Hampton who has also branched out into adult fiction.

Tracey and Simon do their level best to match the strength of the big boys by producing high quality, planet-friendly products in an ever competitive market and thankfully, they are lucky enough to represent some great authors who work hard to promote their writing (an absolute pre-requisite for any ambitious writer).

See MagicOxygen.co.uk/shop for their full range of titles and remember, every single paperback can be ordered from local or national bookshops, and online too.

They actively encourage readers to consider placing orders with small, independent local retailers, which helps keep money in local communities. Magic Oxygen are also very happy to fulfil orders; they might even have a signed edition to hand!

Simon West FRSA
Managing Director Magic Oxygen Ltd
MagicOxygen.co.uk

About The Word Forest Organisation

Empowering Women for Environmental, Economic and Livelihood Improvement.

An 11ᵗʰ Hour Report from the CEO

You wouldn't believe the difficulty I've had writing this...

Despite the fact that the Editor has given me at least 4 weeks' worth of consistently vigorous yet gentle encouragement to scratch out a few creative words for this anthology, I've been utterly devoid of a valid excuse for it being the tardiest article I've ever submitted.

"I just can't write it until we get back from Kenya!" was my recurrent protest.

I didn't want to pen a perfunctory piece about how our work is helping the communities in rural Boré, Coast Province, Kenya, packed with secondhand information (albeit valid and colourful) from our wonderful Project Manager, Alex Katana. Alex is one of the most senior members of the Boré Green Umbrella Co-operative (BGU), the on-the-ground partners who implement our tree planting and classroom building.

I wanted to wait and see what the Magic Oxygen Literary Prize and The Word Forest Organisation had achieved over there, with my own eyes. I wanted to tell the story of the writing contest that jump-started me into creating an environmental charity, in *my* words. I also needed to choose the next half dozen schools we're going to build too; frequent commuting is not on my list of things to do.

Yet here I sit, a clear 7 days in recovery from the most emotionally exhausting, heart warming, mind expanding, soul enriching, positively humbling trip to Kenya, and I am *still* lost for words.

It's not that I don't have any, I have too many; *that's* the problem.

We're Going to Need a Bigger Clipboard

Towards the end of 2017, I was absolutely blown away to receive a donation of ring-fenced funds allowing two of my Trustees and I to undertake a monitoring and evaluation trip to Boré. When you run a charity, you have to take credible, accurate measurements of the impact of your work to show your benefactors and corporate partners, and quite rightly so. The only issue is our beneficiaries are 4,493.84 miles away as the weaver bird flies, give or take.

During the 2½ weeks Ru Hartwell, Simon West and I spent in Kenya, our schedule was jam-packed, you couldn't have squeezed a bus ticket in between appointments and we measured our impact with bells on. We carried out our duties whilst residing with the creatures, and in the comforts, of the Boré Community Forest Centre. It's an impressively positioned, traditionally constructed, circular accommodation block for 14 people that nestles affectionately alongside a similarly sized communal building that has the same huge, round makuti roof but has open walls that invite a welcome breeze to pass through it; quite the perfect place to experience sunup or sundown with a simple revolution of your chair.

The location of this incredible centre is undeniably enviable. It's 3 degrees south of the equator, perched majestically on the absolute edge of a clifftop that delivers a jaw-dropping view out over a colossal natural depression. The land has literally fallen away to reveal a vast

156

sandstone canyon filled with jagged gorges, all layered with slices of pink, orange, white and blood-red crimson rocks.

The local Giriama folk believe it's a sacred space and they call it 'Nyari', 'the place broken by itself'. If you look up a tourist attraction just a few miles away called Hell's Kitchen in Marafa, you'll understand in a heartbeat how it won its name.

The centre has been 11 years in the making and is now a prized community asset. I'm proud to say it's the brainchild of our amazing Trustee and forestry expert, Ru Hartwell. Ru's non-profit company, Community Carbon Link, was the organisation that Magic Oxygen used to plant the first trees that resulted from entries to MOLP 1. Ru has invested his own blood, sweat and tears into many projects with the

BGU over much of the last decade and his local knowledge is second to none; how blessed we are to have him in our fold.

As if our trip to Kenya weren't already exciting enough, our team were actually the first guests to stay in the Forest Centre and a big red ribbon was officially cut by the Hon Peter Ziro Ngowa, Member of the County Assembly, Garashi Ward, on the 27th February, to mark its opening. My word, what an incredible day that was, I shall never forget it! 744 locals put on their most colourful finery and joined us for the largest celebration the community had ever experienced. There were speeches, *lots* of speeches (even I gave a speech) followed by some legendary Giriama dancing and singing from men, women and children, from miles around.

These people know how to party and after over 4 hours of assorted revelry, the food was finally served to the delight of hundreds of hungry, incredibly patient children. I remember seeing the cooking pots arrive at the centre at 7am that morning, on the back of a tiny piki-piki (motorbike). They were easily 4ft wide, a foot and a half deep and the spoons to stir them were the size of a boat's oar. Perfect vessels to cook up and honour the 3 goats they'd sacrificed, served with cabbage, onion, garlic, tomato, rice and wari to mop it all up. Wari is Giriama for the Swahili named dish of ugali, a starchy foodstuff made of flour milled from maize, millet or sorghum, sometimes mixed with cassava flour and cooked in boiling water or milk to form a stiff, dough-like consistency; think malleable but solid-ish sticky rice and you're about there.

The Forest Centre staff won't forget that day in a hurry either and now we three guinea pigs are out of the way, they're all geared up and ready to accept (a) visitors who want to press life's pause button and observe the birds and wildlife, and (b) students, researchers and volunteers who want to learn about sustainability on the climate change front line of tropical Africa. See BoreForestCentre.org for further information and to book your stay.

Green Belt and Braces

Before we cracked on in Boré, we had an amazing 2 night pit-stop in the country's vibrant capital, Nairobi. We hosted our inaugural tree conference: 'Clear the Air: reforest Kenya 2018' at the Green Belt Movement's Lang'ata Learning Centre in Karen. The GBM is arguably one of the most positively influential environmental NGOs in the whole of Kenya, maybe even Africa, and it was a privilege to spend time there. I couldn't think of a better place to meet up with so many friends who are leading grassroots tree planting groups, and with inspirational individuals who are protecting the forests and doing the same. The environmental energy at our conference, was palpable!

The GBM was founded by Professor Wangari Maathai, back in 1977. Wangari was show-stoppingly extraordinary and she was the first African woman to receive the Nobel Peace Prize for her contribution to sustainable development, democracy and peace. She set the organisation up to help rural Kenyan women who reported that their streams were drying up, their food supply was less secure and they had to walk further and further to get firewood for fuel and fencing. Wangari inspired countless Kenyans 'from the bottom up' and at great personal

cost of vilification and even imprisonment, yet she continued to encourage women to work together to plant trees, earn a living and protect Kenya's natural capital.

Sadly, Wangari is no longer with us, but her courageous fighting spirit lives on in the GBM and the new Chair, Marion Wakanyi Kamau, was a very welcome delegate at our conference. Marion is one busy lady; just after we met, Deputy President William Ruto unveiled her as the head of a 10 member multi-sectoral task force, designed to review forestry management in Kenya. Despite some in the media levelling criticism at its formation, in my view, a non-political, pro-environmental group of forest guardians, is needed now more than ever before... in fact, come to think of it, we could do with these groups worldwide!

(Funnily enough, one of the outcomes of our conference was the sound idea that every government and shadow cabinet should have a Tree Minister. Now there's a great title just waiting to be a trending hashtag!)

Over a cup of tea and a moist-as-you-like butternut squash cake, Marion and I talked about how much has changed since Wangari pulled the topic of Kenya's ever decreasing canopy cover, kicking and screaming into the public arena, over 40 years ago.

"It was contentious then – it still is today", she told me, as she praised our organisation for putting the imperative topic of reforestation in Kenya, back onto the international stage.

I've been very lucky to forge a connection to Wangari's incredible daughter, Wanjira. She continues to fly the flag for women and the environment as Director for the Partnership on Women Entrepreneurship in Renewables (wPOWER) Hub, amongst other great, green roles. Sadly we weren't able to meet during our hectic sojourn to Lang'ata but we did start a little dialogue about the benefit of united energies and maybe working together in Coast Province; more on that when I have it, all my digits are crossed, which is making it really hard to type…

#DroughtKe

The science is simple, the facts are mortifying. Kenya *has* been in drought for the past 5 years, despite the fact that the day before we left to come home on the 4th March, the heavens opened. The Kenyan Meteorological Department were very keen to stress that, "This is *not* the start of the greatly awaited long rains!" They usually appear towards the end of April, but almost a fortnight on from our departure, the Kenyan media are reporting the current death toll at 15 and with rain forecast for the next 5 days at least, it is likely to rise. Many lost their lives in violent flood waters, others in vehicle collisions and also through the collapse of weak buildings.

Then would you believe, just minutes ago, Alex Katana sent an email to inform us that the Sabaki River has burst its banks. It's Kenya's second longest river at 390 km and it drains a basin area of 70,000 km². As I type, 1,000 residents of the Nuru community who live in mud huts on the palm tree-lined banks of the river, have been displaced. They have no money, no homes and no food. Their livelihoods will have been washed away. There are no aid agencies waiting to take care of them either; we are trying to get through to Shelter Box and the Kenya Red Cross to alert them to the crisis and to see if they can help.

One of the local children who we probably met when we visited Mikuyuni Primary School, fell into a flooded toilet pit yesterday and died; I doubt they've made it onto those national statistics.

Simon and I stood on the bone dry river bed of the Sabaki River just a few weeks ago. The sand was so hot and the ingress of its burning grains through the holes in my sandals, seared my feet. On the river bed itself, there were countless diamond like sparkles and you could see them glinting all the way across the 500ft wide dust bed of a river. There was a thin strip of dirty water trickling through the centre of the Sabaki and some of the locals were digging deep holes in the sand

around it, trying desperately to extract a few buckets of uncontaminated water for their families and livestock. Whilst I stood there and recorded a brief interview, 100 thirsty cattle trekked down past our camera, making a beeline for the most precious commodity of all; the water.

Kenya is massively underprepared for extreme weather eventualities and mass human displacement and to be honest, so is the UK! While our team were baking in higher than usual temperatures in Boré before the rain arrived, our friends and families back in the UK were being immobilised by snow storms as the Beast from the East wreaked havoc and bought the country to a virtual standstill. At much the same time, central parts of the US were also struggling with melting snow and persistent rain from their own relentless storms, which resulted in catastrophic flooding and the wettest February ever recorded in Louisville, Pittsburgh and Indiana as 70 rivers reached flood capacity. Yet in the Arctic, temperatures were logged 30C higher than normal as a different type of storm propelled significant heat through the Greenland Sea.

Back in 2015, the Kenya Meteorological Department said that 'Occurrences of heavy rain and flooding would be frequent due to the expected evolution of global sea surface temperatures, that is favourable for the development of a weak El Niño.'

Climate change *is* real, extreme weather events are occurring all over the globe and whether or not you believe it is being exacerbated by our activities; we living, breathing two legged creatures are going to have to shake one of those legs and work out better ways to deal with them.

In the view of countless eminent scientists, environmentalists, naturalists, tree planters and just plain old ordinary awake optimists like me #TreesAreTheKey to helping reduce the chaos caused by some of the problems. They do soak up CO_2 from the atmosphere. Their very existence helps slow down catastrophic run off from floods. They could encourage the normal rains to come back to Kenya and their mass planting throughout Kenya could help to prevent her desertification.

I don't profess to having all the answers, but I do know that planting new trees and protecting the existing canopy cover in Kenya and across the planet for that matter, is vital to our very existence.

Kenya's drought has gripped them in a death-like vice for 5 clear years, during which the maize crops in our region have repeatedly failed; maize farming used to provide a stable, reliable way of earning a living in Coast Province. The calamitous reality of sitting in the back of the project car, a thoroughly dilapidated 18 year old jeep, observing field after field of drought-crippled, dead excuses for failed crops, is gut-wrenching, particularly when you know that if a family fails to make a living from growing it, they are highly likely to turn to other desperate measures to make ends meet; making illegal charcoal and prostituting their children, being two repellant, common backstops.

Charcoal: Black Death to the Forest

Creating charcoal for the black market has been an underbelly necessity for too long and it's the very last thing our communities want to do - they absolutely recognise the environmental value of trees and whilst there isn't a Giriama phrase to accurately describe CO_2, hewa chafu (dirty air) is just fine. You don't need any language skills to express the welcome relief found in the shade of a magnificent baobab tree.

I learned how to spot a baobab on day one, with its thick, swollen base of a trunk which forms a massive caudex and gives it a bulbous, bottle-like appearance. Baobab's have been carbon dated at over 1,000 years old, undoubtedly all down to that gargantuan trunk which can store up to 120,000 litres of water, hydrating it through the most horrific periods of drought. No wonder they call it the Tree of Life; who on earth would want to fell something that incredible for fuel? Someone caught between a rock and a hard place, is the answer.

Making charcoal might net a few desperately needed Kenyan Shillings to stop your family from starving but it is an unequivocally nefarious deed. An illegally sold 25kg sack would usually make someone about 600 KSH / £4. For further context, it costs around 60 bob / 40p to cook up 3 family sized meals using charcoal. During our stay, the government announced a serious countrywide crackdown on this shady industry responsible for removing the very thing Kenya needs in order to help restore the normal rains again. Unfortunately, the ongoing management of the ban is way past complicated and the black market price for that 600 KSH sack, has just risen to 3,000 KSH / £21.

Just to add another difficulty to the mix, there are lots of *legal* logging and charcoal businesses and they are struggling with the government impositions too, as vigilant activists are on the hawkeyed lookout for any transportation or movement of the BBQ fuel that has found itself wrapped in international notoriety; however you cut it, this situation clearly isn't going to resolve itself anytime soon.

    I had a very interesting chat about this with the Senior Chief of Garashi Location, Ndundi Chula Ndundi. I asked him if there were any government provisions in place for people who were ensnared in the charcoal industry, to help them get out of it. He said they've long recognised it's an issue and there are currently three solutions available: there are two types of loan and (apparently) there's a grant too. These are all designed to provide cash to set up an alternative legal enterprise. I'm trying to find out more about how viable they are and to see what hoops of fire one has to leap through in order to qualify. The trouble with living in the serious bush in a place like Boré, is there are no walk in advice centres and my worry is that our remote community might not even be aware of the fact they exist.

A Woman's Work

Midway through our trip, I spent an indescribably magical day interviewing a group of local women with kind assistance from an amazing translator called Karembo. With the aid of her gentle, softly spoken voice that wrapped itself around every difficult sentence like it was cotton wool, I girded my loins and prepared myself for poignant facts. What I actually got was staggering and incogitable information and I had no idea the knowledge was going to impact my life in quite the way it did.

We 15 women gathered together, sat tentatively and quietly at first, around large tables in the blessed shade of the forest centre's communal space, looking out over the Nyari. Predictable refreshing wisps of wind

usually rose and lipped over the clifftop by around 10am and I was appreciative of every one of them as they temporarily cooled the layer of moisture that coated every inch of my skin.

I was very grateful for the kind assistance of the local women with my research, particularly as I knew many of them had walked several miles to come and see me through early-morning temperatures that were rocking up towards 30 degrees. I started the session by requesting that Edward, our amazing multi-talented assistant at the centre, prepare the women some fresh fruit. I must admit, I got more than a few looks from a couple of the men who were hanging around to ensure that the women didn't roll out tales about evil husbands who mistreated them. The looks intensified when I said that all the women would require a good lunch too. "But what will *you* have to eat if we give them all the food?" was the initial response. "Not as much, or maybe we'll just go buy some more vegetables!" was my reply.

Edward was incredibly obliging and so very happy to help with anything we needed. He's a young father of two and a deputy pastor at the local church – we saw him preach and man, he rocked it. He had very good spoken and written English and he taught me a daily line or two of Giriama and Swahili. With the distinct lack of any local shops to pop to for bits and pieces and no on-site washing machine, Edward had great forethought and he attended to all these things and more, retiring a short while before we went to bed and arriving around 7am, often with a bowl of freshly cooked chapatis for breakfast. To be honest, our work schedule was so full and what with travelling in the back of the jeep for miles on end, I reached filthy o'clock within 5 minutes anyway. I was happy to just recycle the less grubby clothes, as the abundant, unavoidable red dust that inserted itself into every fibre of my outfits, could only be removed by an Edward wash.

As he prepared their food, I started an exchange of information with the women by investing them with my story, explaining a bit about my life and what had brought me to Boré. All they knew of me up to this point, was I was the 'mzungu' who'd funded some of the school buildings nearby and the planting of some trees too.

Are You Sitting Comfortably?

I took a deep breath and rolled it right back: my mother had been alcohol dependent and my early years had been volatile and tumultuous. I'd endured a nauseating divorce but I had three amazing children to show for it and thankfully, I'd gone on to find a wonderful man and remarried. There were copious smiles of empathy and understanding, as domestic abuse is sadly all too common over there and the media frequently talks about the male dominated alcohol epidemic in Kenya, especially in the widespread use and abuse of illicit brews; speaking of which, one night later that week I had occasion to try about a teaspoon of palm wine. It was a particularly disgusterous, yeasty concoction that smelled like a bakers armpit and it probably had the power to remove paint. It's easy enough to make apparently and no doubt delivers a cheap kick #CaseInPoint

The interviews went phenomenally well and whilst it was a bit of a shock to learn they didn't really know each other very well at the start, the picture they eventually painted was analogous. They hadn't realised they were such kindred spirits, whose lives were similarly braided by threads of relentless toil, fatigue, obligation and encumbrance, not to mention dire inequality, yet their indomitable spirits prevailed.

I learned about their struggles with all manner of indigenous issues and soon realised they consider them to be simple matters of fact in their everyday lives, however, I think their hardships are intensely magnified by their circumstances and environment. They rise at 4am, 2 hours before dawn, to walk several miles to fetch water in 20 litre jerry cans which they carry back skilfully on their heads through the bush, dodging a selection of Kenya's 171 species of snake, many of which are deadly. These huge plastic containers are unbelievably arduous things to walk with, God knows, I tried it and it's virtually impossible to look down to check for snakes! Their weight alone leaves the women prone to suffering with musculoskeletal disorders and other related disabilities. Oh, and at the moment, there are two lions on the loose in the area too - early morning is hunting time.

The women collect all the firewood for heat and cooking and carry it back in a weighty 'head lot'. They get the kids to school and if they've time, some are allowed to work but they don't always get to see their wages as they money frequently goes straight to their husbands; women rarely have bank accounts.

Not a single woman bemoaned their lot in life and believe me, they had more than enough to carp about. Conversely, they were completely oblivious of their inherent, phenomenal capabilities, their unacquired wherewithal, their valiant resilience and their resolute ability to cope

with just about anything life had to throw at them.

Women prop up the familial backbones in Kenyan society. They are the shufflers of children, the creators of food, the keepers of house. They are also underrepresented in politics and by the decision makers, they have less access to education, land and employment. Add to this an insufferable lack of hygienic solutions to cope with periods, the overshadowing threat of FGM and sexual diseases introduced by wayward husbands and it's easy to understand why social isolation and depression bite rural Kenyan women hard.

I was astounded by the humility and positivity of the women I spoke to and it was interesting to note that over the course of the day, their body language shifted from reserved and quiet, to congenial, convivial and at times, positively giggly. As you can imagine, lunch went down a treat and it was made even more wonderful when Edward came out with a jug of water and a bowl and washed each of the women's hands before they ate.

One of the most shocking conversations I had with them was about menstruation. Some of them have occasional access to disposables, but most use cut up rags, some use leaves. I deliberately took over a washable sanitary pad that clips around your underwear to hold it in place – the women had never seen anything like it before – one of them is a seamstress and she was tasked to cut it up to make a pattern.

If you'd like to help us continue to expand this group, please make a donation to our charity by visiting WordForest.org/donate. Any amount will help! Your money will pay for their meal, their water, their saplings, their time and care to nurture them and to buy new seeds for the nursery. It will also pay for us to buy some fabric so we can get to work running up a few washable pads to give these wonderful women some comfort and dignity during their period and it'll undoubtedly improve their mental and general health and wellbeing too.

Support the Women - Help the Whole Planet

Wednesday 21st March marks my 52nd birthday. It's also the 8th International Day of Forests and it'll mark the very first meeting of the women's tree planting and empowerment group that I set up as a result of my interviews with them. The group will be facilitated by Karembo's sister, Florence, who will be ably assisted by Esther, one of the women's representatives at the BGU. Everyone will meet at the Forest Centre to enjoy a lunch, some fruit and fresh, uncontaminated water to drink, all taken care of by our dear friend, Edward.

I learned a long time ago that in our community it's basically the women who do most of the work in the tree nurseries. That said, the BGU, which comprises 2/3 men, is working hard to increase the number of women in the group and they are very respectful of women's rights and equality. This is remarkably forward thinking for rural Kenya, and we are delighted that the men see this group as a positive new initiative. They understand that it will be of direct benefit to the health and well-being of the women, which will have an uplifting impact on the whole community and it has their full support.

Our group will enable women to get together to simply 'be' and to share top tips on best practice for looking after the forest and protecting the existing canopy cover. They'll expand their environmental knowledge by having access to global news and by seeing what's going on in the forests throughout Kenya, as Florence has use of a laptop kindly donated by one of our supporters. Perhaps most importantly of all, they'll be given a few saplings to plant and they'll receive money *in their hands* for doing so; Wangari Maathai's dream will live on in Boré.

Ultimately, the group will get more trees in the ground which will eventually lift them out of poverty; everyone's a winner, including Mother Nature.

Find out what happened during our visits to the forests and schools by subscribing to our news feed at WordForest.org and if your looking for a way to support our work, sign up as a one of our valued members!

Tracey West FRSA
CEO & Fundraiser The Word Forest Organisation

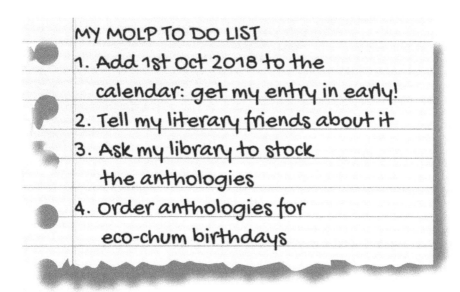

MY MOLP TO DO LIST
1. Add 1st Oct 2018 to the
   calendar: get my entry in early!
2. Tell my literary friends about it
3. Ask my library to stock
   the anthologies
4. Order anthologies for
   eco-chum birthdays

Lightning Source UK Ltd.
Milton Keynes UK
UKHW02f1921280318
320194UK00006B/36/P